DEEP INTO THE GOLD MINE

"Turn and run for it, lads!" he yelled.

Rifle fire sounded from back in the tunnel. One of the Cornishmen grabbed his leg and slipped into the hole, yelling as he fell. The echoes died out when there was a loud *sploosh* way below.

The others scrambled toward the main tunnel, the sulfurous smell choking them. They were just rounding the corner into the new shaft when an explosion tore through the side tunnel, hurling dust and rocks through the mine.

"Buffalo Brothers" adventures from Tor Books

Colorado Gold
Jayhawker Crossing

COLORADO GOLD

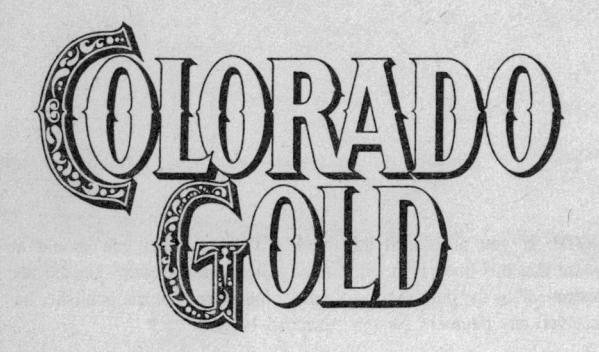

JACK STANFORD

A TOM DOHERTY ASSOCIATES BOOK
NEW YORK

NOTE: If you purchased this book without a cover you should be aware that this book is stolen property. It was reported as "unsold and destroyed" to the publisher, and neither the author nor the publisher has received any payment for this "stripped book."

This is a work of fiction. All the characters and events portrayed in this book are fictitious, and any resemblance to real people or events is purely coincidental.

COLORADO GOLD

Copyright © 1995 by Earl Murray

All rights reserved, including the right to reproduce this book, or portions thereof, in any form.

Cover art by Royo

A Tor Book
Published by Tom Doherty Associates, Inc.
175 Fifth Avenue
New York, N.Y. 10010

Tor® is a registered trademark of Tom Doherty Associates, Inc.

ISBN: 0-812-53402-6

First edition: January 1995

Printed in the United States of America

0 9 8 7 6 5 4 3 2 1

To Paul, who has found his
fortune in Colorado.

One

The midday sun shone like fire through a windswept sky. The air was filled with sand blown like shards of glass across the open plains.

A lone horseman on a stout buckskin rode with his bandanna protecting his face and his hat low over his eyes. Joel McCann had been in the saddle for over twenty-four hours. He cared little about the sand and heat. He had a destination, and he would stay on his horse until he reached it.

McCann had just crossed the Texas border, into New Mexico Territory. He rode on until he could see a grove of paloverde, waving like large shadows in the wind and dust.

He had reached the Cimarron River. He knew that a few adobe buildings stood among the trees, the only settlement for miles in any direction.

The tiny village of Carminga lay along the Cimarron Cutoff, a shortcut along the Santa Fe Trail. In years past, the trail had been used by fur traders moving in and out of Taos. Now it was just a quicker way to reach the growing Southwest, or travel on into California.

The road was shorter, but the chances of dying from thirst or thieves was much greater. For McCann, Carminga was his journey's end, the place where he was to meet an old friend.

McCann was already three days late in reaching Carminga. He hoped Corky Devlin had not given up hope.

Coming down from Colorado, the telegraph from Devlin had said. *Will meet you on 1 May in Carminga where we spoke in the small saloon two years past. Will save the details for then. You won't be disappointed at the news I bring.*

McCann had gotten the telegraph in Fort Worth, where he spent what little time he wasn't in the saddle. Corky Devlin was someone Joel McCann could not disappoint. They had fought together during the southern rebellion, what folks were now calling the Civil War.

Though Devlin was unpredictable at best, McCann looked upon him as more than a brother. Devlin had saved his life during the last battle at Bull Run. McCann had fallen and Devlin had stood over him and kept the onslaught of blue from overrunning them.

Despite his wounds, McCann had gotten to his feet and had continued to fight.

"You'd best sit yourself down, lad, and save what strength you've got," Devlin had insisted. "You're no help, you know, and I've got more to do than save your butt all the day long!"

Devlin had saved his life not just once that day, but three times.

Four years had passed since the end of the war. McCann had spent the entire time trying to forget what he had seen and felt, and what he had lost.

He had not wanted to join the Confederacy but had been told it was either wear the colors or go to prison for stealing cattle. Though he had stolen no livestock from anyone, he had marched into battle.

This had come less than a year into his marriage to Minnie Storm, his childhood sweetheart. He had also left behind his ten-month-old son, Clint.

Now every mile he rode and every town he came to, he thought about them. He had returned from the war to find them gone—taken, it was said, by thieves.

Joel McCann spent every spare moment searching. He would never stop until he found his wife and son, dead or alive. He needed to know, one way or another.

McCann now hoped that the telegraph had something to do with his lost family. Had Devlin met them somewhere? He had shown Devlin their photographs many times during the war. Maybe Devlin had found them settled somewhere in Colorado Territory. A thousand possibilities ran through his mind.

As he neared the edge of town, McCann pulled his Colt Navy .44 and spun the cylinder. He also made certain that the action on his Henry rifle worked smoothly.

The war had not been good to him, nor had the years since. He had fought to save himself many times. He had learned to be cautious, no matter how peaceful his surroundings looked.

Carminga lay dormant, except for three horses tied in front of the lone saloon, called the Mockingbird. A small boardinghouse sat nearby, seemingly vacant, as was the livery stable just beyond.

McCann dismounted and led his buckskin to a watering trough at one of the hitching posts. The trees offered welcome shelter against the wind, the only shelter McCann had found in his two full days of riding.

McCann dusted himself off with his hat and stepped into the saloon. The inside was dark and smelled of smoke and spilled whiskey. In one corner, near a small window, was a barber pole.

An old man lay sleeping under a table near the pole, snoring loudly. Three men played cards along one wall. They looked up from their game and stared.

A bartender stood, polishing glasses. He was small and stooped over, in late middle age, with long sideburns and a thick, flowing mustache.

He turned and studied McCann. "Help you?"

"Let's start with whiskey and water back."

"Whatever you'd like." The bartender poured water into a coffee cup from a jug along the back bar. He filled a shot glass, then watched McCann down the whiskey and pour the water after it, smacking his lips. He set out the shot glass for another.

The bartender poured, his hands shaking. "Need a shave and haircut? I'll wake him up."

"Not today," McCann replied. "Maybe another time."

The bartender went back to polishing glasses. It was quiet, but for the wind outside and the barber's snoring. The three men at the table continued to stare.

"The town seems pretty empty," McCann remarked.

"Drying up," the bartender said. "Nobody will stay and run the boardinghouse and livery. I can't do it all myself."

"Maybe you should get some women," one of the men at the table said. "I've been wanting one for a while." The other two laughed.

"I tried that," the bartender said. "They don't stay on. They ride out with somebody first chance they get."

McCann studied the three men. Two of them looked enough alike to be brothers. They wore similar hats and clothing and were light-complected, well into their thirties, with slim faces and quick, darting eyes.

The third one, who wanted a woman, was large and dark, and younger than the brothers. He wore a battered Stetson, tipped back. He was rocking on his chair. His nose was hooked to one side and his heavy beard was filled with dust.

The bartender drew water from a pump at the end of the bar and filled a jug. He poured more water for McCann.

"It's a bad day for riding," he said. His hands were shaking. "It's the breath of hell itself out there."

"I'm here on purpose," McCann said.

The bartender laughed nervously. "That so. I figured you were lost."

"I'm looking for a man about this tall." McCann held his hand out at shoulder height. "His name's

Devlin. Corky Devlin. He's about ten years older than me, built strong, and wears a red derby hat."

The bartender's eyes shifted to the three men at the table, and back to McCann. "A red derby?" His hands shook even more.

"Yeah. It might be a little dusty, but it's red. You wouldn't mistake it."

The three men at the table began whispering. The bartender looked toward them and went back to wiping glasses, but his hands shook so violently that, after dropping two, he gave up.

"He should have come in here a couple or three days back," McCann said. "I don't know. Maybe he's not gotten here yet."

"Haven't seen nobody like that," the bartender said. "Nobody in a red derby. You're right, he must not have come yet." His eyes again went to the three at the table.

McCann turned to the table. "How about it? Any of you seen someone who fits that description?"

The big one turned from his cards. He smiled at McCann, exposing a large gap in his teeth. "Nobody in a red hat would stay in here for very long. I wouldn't let him." He laughed.

The other two snickered. One of the brothers, older and slightly larger, looked up quickly to see McCann, leaning back with his elbows on the bar, staring hard at the big man.

"You say you don't like red hats?" McCann asked.

"Leon was just funning you, that's all," the brother told McCann. "Weren't you, Leon?"

"He's right. I don't like red hats," the big man said. "I won't let anybody stay here if they wear red hats. That's the way it is."

"You know something," McCann told the big man, "this hat I'm wearing, it used to be red. It used to be bright red."

The big man laughed. "No, that's not a red hat."

"Sure it is," McCann said. "Are you blind?"

The big man's smile disappeared. "What did you say?"

"I told you that I wear red hats," McCann said, still leaning back. "If this one doesn't look red to you, then you're blind."

The big man slid his chair back. The bartender retreated to the far end of the bar. The older brother leaned over toward the big man.

"Don't. There's another way."

McCann eased off the bar, his arms falling loosely at his sides, his right hand near the butt of his Colt. "Yeah, I'm sure of it. I'd have to say you're blind. And stupid to boot."

The two brothers stood up quickly. "Leon, it's time to go," the older brother said. "I already told you that."

The big man stood up and shook them off. "No. I've got business with this red-hat man first."

"We don't need any shooting, Leon," the younger brother said. "Say good-bye to the stranger and we'll be on our way."

"I can take him."

McCann was watching the other two as closely as he watched the big man. Neither of them seemed to be anxious to fight, but you never knew.

"I'm going to take him," the big man repeated.

"Forget it, Leon," the older brother demanded. "Let's go."

"You two go. I'll come later."

"Leon, we'll come back another time."

"Yeah," the younger brother said. "We'll come back again. Soon."

"I'm not ready to go yet."

"Leon, you aren't listening," the older brother insisted.

The big man studied the brothers. "Oh, I see." He was smiling. "Yes, we'll go." He started for the door behind the brothers. "Enjoy your stay, red-hat man. I'll be seeing you again sometime."

"Maybe," McCann said.

Two

As soon as the three had left the saloon, McCann pulled his Colt and turned the table sideways, spilling the cards and chips onto the floor. He took cover behind it.

The bartender was crouched behind the bar, trembling. Outside, the wind whined. Inside, the old barber snored and McCann cocked his pistol.

The three burst into the saloon, shooting wildly. The big man and the older brother were in front. McCann fired two shots into the older brother, knocking him backward. He fell over the sleeping barber, who raised his head momentarily.

The older brother crawled along the floor and sat up against the wall, holding his chest, looking around with a dazed expression. The younger brother slid behind the bar, while the big man sprayed bullets into the table where McCann was crouched, yelling, "I'll kill you, red-hat man! I'll kill you!"

Wood splinters flew everywhere. McCann rolled away, a bullet grazing his right shoulder. He came to one knee and fanned his Colt. Bullets slammed into the big man, turning him in a half circle.

He fell sideways into the bar. The pistol in his left hand discharged and fell to the floor. The big man caught himself, holding his heavy body up with his left elbow, and turned around.

McCann talked from behind the table. "You had enough?" he asked the big man, watching for the younger brother to come up over the bar.

The big man stared at his chest. Blood was staining the front of his shirt. He slowly raised his remaining pistol. "Red-hat man. I'm going to ... shoot you."

McCann aimed over the table and fired. The bullet slammed into the big man's forehead. He dropped like a huge sack of flour, thudding heavily to the floor.

Gunfire came from over the bar, splintering the table and nearby chairs. McCann ducked behind another table and reloaded quickly. He heard the younger brother's boots as he ran from the saloon. Soon he was kicking his horse into a dead run out of town.

The older brother, still seated against the wall, began to laugh.

McCann stood up. The room was filled with smoke and the smell of death. He approached the older brother cautiously, while the man stared at him and continued to laugh.

"You see this as funny?" McCann asked him.

He coughed and wiped blood from his mouth. "I can't cry."

"Who are you?"

"It doesn't matter now. I'm dead."

"You make bad choices, sooner or later it'll catch up with you."

"Save your religion speech."

"What's this all about?" McCann asked.

The man ignored him. He was shaking his head. "I knew we should've waited." His face twisted into a frown. "Any other time would've been better. That stupid DuCain!" He coughed again. "Now look ... look at what's happened." His chin dropped and he fell sideways, air escaping from his lungs.

The bartender came out from behind the bar and stared at the bodies.

"You're a deadly man."

"I've got some questions for you, mister," McCann said. He walked toward the bartender, his pistol still drawn, but pointed toward the floor.

The bartender raised his hands. "Don't shoot. Please! I had no part in it. I swear!"

"Did you know any of these men?"

"Not any of them. I swear. They came in yesterday. I didn't know them, I swear."

"You've seen Corky Devlin, the man in the red derby, though, haven't you? I could tell by the way you acted. You and these men knew who I was talking about, didn't you?"

"Yes, but I had no part in it. I swear!"

"No part in what? What are you talking about?"

"Listen, they told me they'd cut me in on the deal. If I just went along with them, I'd get a share. But I told them I didn't want no part of it."

"What are you talking about?"

"The gold. They talked about the gold."

"What gold? Make some sense, bartender. What are you talking about?"

"Listen, maybe you should talk to your friend." The bartender pointed to the back door. "There's a shed behind. Your friend's in there. The red-derby man's in there."

"Back there? In a shed? Why?"

"They put him in there," the bartender said. "Please, just let me go."

McCann squinted at him. "What are you afraid of?"

"I just figured those men would kill me," the bartender said. "Now I figure you will. I don't want to die."

McCann pointed. "Hand me that jug of water."

The bartender hurried behind the bar. He struggled, his hands shaking violently. McCann reached out and grabbed the jug.

The bartender pointed toward the back. "He's in the shed. You'll find him easy enough."

"You'll take me back there," McCann insisted. "I don't want to have to use my gun again."

"No, no. You won't have to. You won't. I'll take you."

The bartender led the way out the back door, turning his head often to see if McCann was preparing to shoot him. McCann, who had holstered his Colt, became increasingly disgusted.

"You're lucky I don't wring your neck, mister."

"Nothing against you, I swear," the bartender said. "But those three, they would've killed me sure."

"How could you think they'd make a deal with you, for gold or anything else?"

"I just don't want to die, mister. That's all."

The bartender opened the door to a small adobe shed and pointed inside. As McCann peered in, the bartender began running through the alley.

McCann let him go and stepped into the shed. On the floor sat Corky Devlin, bound and gagged, wearing his famous red derby. His eyes widened.

McCann pulled the gag free and began to untie him. "I didn't expect this, Corky. Fine way to spend an afternoon."

Devlin wiped his brow and reached for the water. "Damn, it's hot! And that wind. Did you ever see the likes of it?" He drank greedily, until McCann slowed him down.

"Not too fast, Corky. There's plenty of water and plenty of time now."

"I'm beholden to you, Joel. I'm about cooked, I am."

"Would you like to tell me about this?" McCann asked.

Devlin noticed the crease along the top of McCann's shoulder. "I heard the shooting. I wasn't worried about you, though, Joel. Not a-tall. You're one for getting in and out of scrapes, you are.... Of course, I've helped on occasion. You'll grant me that."

"Granted. Now you'll consider this as a payback."

"You'll get no argument from me. I've saved you three times, though. You've got two left."

"Let's not rush things," McCann said. "How did you get into all this in the first place?"

"By sending you the wire," Devlin replied.

"That's how it all began. I told the man operating the telegraph about our good fortune, and he must have told Mr. Hurlan. Then Mr. Hurlan, fiend that he is, sent those three after me."

"Mr. Hurlan?"

Devlin gulped more water. "Marvin Hurlan. He wants our gold!"

"Our gold?"

"That's what I wired you about, Joel. Yes, we're rich, we are. You and me, lad. We've got gold in the Colorado Rockies. A great mountain of gold, lad!"

McCann frowned. "Are you talking about that claim we put in together ten years back? That's hardly worth all this."

"The very same one. And it is worth all this."

"I thought you told me during the war that the claim was a bust."

"Ah, but it was then. Times have changed, Joel. Times have changed. True, there wasn't much surface gold where we had our claim, but I'll tell you, there's a lode underground, a mother lode at that."

"I don't know anything about underground mining," McCann said. "Nor do you."

"We can learn, lad," Devlin insisted. "There's new ways of getting the gold out of the rock. There's mills a-popping up like trees everywhere. A railroad's planned to come up from Denver."

"A railroad?" McCann said. "I didn't think that country would ever come alive again."

"It's true, the place died down for a good time," Devlin said. "But you'd ought to see it now. You'd really ought to see it now. That's why those three came after me."

"Tell me now, who's Marvin Hurlan?" McCann asked.

Colorado Gold   15

"He's a businessman in Central City who's investing in the new railroad," Devlin replied. "He came up from Denver. Now he's looking for the good claims in the area. He'll do anything to take them. I guess I should've known he'd want ours to boot."

"So he sent hired killers after you," McCann said. "He didn't want you getting back to Central City?"

"He didn't want *either* of us getting back there, lad. You should know that by now. I rode the back trails, in case someone followed me, but they were here waiting when I rode into town. The telegraph man must've told Hurlan everything."

"You must've told the telegraph man everything," McCann said. "Don't you know better than that?"

"Oh, but, Joel, lad, I was so happy for the two of us, and nobody else to share it with. But you're right, I opened me mouth, and I'm sorry for that."

"I don't know why they didn't kill you right away," McCann said. "I don't know why they bothered to tie you up."

"Because I lied to them, Joel," Devlin said. "I told them you had a map to another diggings, and that we were planning on filing more claims. They wanted to learn about that, you see."

"What?"

"I had to tell them something, Joel. Otherwise they would've killed me sure. You just said it. They would have killed me right away. We couldn't have that, now could we? After all, we've got to mine that gold together."

"Two of them won't be killing anyone now."

"The two brothers," Devlin continued, "the Carltons, are the worst kind of killers. Hurlan uses them a lot. Folks in the diggings know about them."

"There's only one of them left," McCann told him. "I got one of the brothers and the big man."

"Leon DuCain. The big, dirty one. That's good to know. Which one of the brothers did you get?"

"The bigger one. He looked to be the older."

Devlin frowned. "Len Carlton. It would have been better to have gotten Lon, the little brother. That it would. But we can't be a-fretting over that, now can we?"

McCann went to the door. The wind was still blowing strongly. Devlin drank more water and began rubbing the circulation back into his hands and feet.

"They tied me up proper, they did. I'd like to do the same to them."

"There's only one left, Corky. Remember?"

"Ah, that's right. Thanks for reminding me. I'll sleep lots better, I will. Lon Carlton is worse than the other two combined, he is."

"I wonder where he went," McCann said. "And I don't trust that bartender."

"Ah! Don't worry none about that bartender. He's likely still running. Most spineless fiend I ever laid eyes on."

"They're the kind who'll shoot you in the back," McCann pointed out. "I'd like to rest a little, over in that boardinghouse, but I don't want him sneaking up on me."

"You'd fare better to worry about Lon Carlton," Devlin said. "But I'll keep an eye open while you rest. It's the least I can do for you." He rose to his feet and stumbled. "I feel a little faint."

"You drank too much water. Sit down a minute."

"I'll sit in the boardinghouse. I can't stand the likes of this shed any longer, nor this little town, for that matter. I'd never take holidays here, you can bet on that."

McCann helped Devlin to the door. "You picked this place. Why would you want to come all the way down here? You could have told me the news in the telegram. You told everyone else."

"I had another surprise for you, lad," Devlin said. "It was about your family, your wife and son."

"You found them?"

"Well, I had learned they were in this country. But I couldn't be certain. I'm still not certain. You get your rest and we'll travel on."

"I don't care much about resting now. I'd as soon look for my family."

"We can't go in this wind," Devlin remarked. "Besides, you need the rest. Your eyes are about puffed shut."

McCann helped Devlin through the back door and into the saloon. Flies were collecting on the bodies in large numbers. The barber lay on the floor, still asleep.

Devlin looked around and shook his head. "This place is a mess. I'd say the bartender had best get to work."

"I figure the younger brother will be back to bury his kin," McCann said. "Maybe we can end our relationship with him then."

Devlin slipped behind the bar and selected a couple of bottles. "It's even odds either way, I'd say. Lon Carlton looks after himself and cares about nothing or no one else." He popped the cork on one and took a long swallow. "If I was a betting man, I'd say you're right. He'll be back. But I never bet. You know that, lad."

McCann started for the door. "I'm going to the boardinghouse. I'll get some rest. And we'll go."

Devlin grabbed a third bottle and stuck it under his arm. He took another drink and stopped beside the sleeping barber. "Maybe I'll wake him up later for a shave."

"How about if I give you a shave?" McCann suggested. "I'll bet my hand is steadier."

"Ah, but you got me there, lad." He took one last look around the saloon and took a deep breath. "All this in the name of riches. 'Tis a pity, isn't it?" He winked at McCann. "Not to worry, though, lad. They're our riches, and we'll be using them for a good cause. Eh, lad? For a very good cause."

Three

Lon Carlton rode out from Carminga, leading his brother's horse. The body of Len Carlton lay draped over the saddle. Still dazed from the experience, the younger Carlton was reliving the saloon shootout.

In his mind he could see his brother's surprised look as bullets from the tall gunman's Colt slammed into him, knocking him backwards and into the wall. His brother had turned to him, his eyes saying, *What happened? Can you help me?* But there had been nothing the younger Carlton could do.

And DuCain had also fallen. *I've got business with this red-hat man . . . business with this red-hat man.* The words haunted Lon Carlton. That stupid DuCain! Why couldn't he let it go? Why couldn't he wait and do it the right way? No, he had had to try and prove himself. It had cost them dearly.

Lon Carlton still couldn't accept that his brother was dead. It seemed so unreal. He had watched a lot of men die, and had killed many of them himself, but he had never thought he would live to see the day when his older brother would be gunned down by someone else.

Carlton rode through the late afternoon, into evening, finally stopping in the twilight. At the top of a low rise, he dismounted and took a spyglass from his saddlebag.

On his belly, he surveyed a small arroyo below, where a creek flowed peacefully. He never stopped anywhere for anytime, no matter how quiet everything seemed, without looking things over from a distance.

The arroyo was calm. Just a few deer drinking. No better place to bury his brother, he thought, and put the spyglass back into his saddlebag.

In the sky, a half-moon was slowly rising. The day's heat was giving way to a desert breeze, a night wind that flowed down off the Sangre de Cristos and brought a chill to the bones.

Carlton untied a small shovel from his saddle. He and his brother had never gone anywhere without taking the little shovels. Gold could be anywhere. But what good was gold now?

As Carlton dug, he thought about the tall gunfighter and his cool manner. The man had challenged the three of them without so much as a second thought.

Joel McCann. That was the name on the mining claim that Marvin Hurlan wanted. The name McCann, and also that of C.F. Devlin, the little man in the red derby.

Hurlan wanted their gold claim bad enough to send three men to the northern edge of New Mexico Territory. Carlton reflected on Hurlan's words: "I don't want either of them leaving Carminga alive. Take care of them down there, and I'll do the rest to get the claims up here."

After the shootout, being the only one left alive, Carlton had ridden from town to gather himself and had returned, thinking seriously about trying to bushwhack the gunman while he was sleeping beneath the trees behind the boardinghouse.

It had been sorely tempting. Devlin seemed to be nothing to worry about. But McCann's sure aim had kept Carlton from following through on his impulse.

Had he gotten a clear shot, revenge would have been sweet. But had he missed or only wounded McCann, things would have been hard. The tall gunman wasn't the kind who would ever give up.

There would be another day, another time, Carlton had thought. He had made the promise to himself and to his brother as he had dragged the body from the saloon and loaded it onto his horse.

There would be a better way for revenge. It would have to be a sure way, a foolproof way, so that Joel McCann would go down for sure, and would not rise again.

Carlton worked to make the hole deep. No wolves would dig his brother up, he would see to it. With each lift of dirt, he further relived the day, wishing that they had done things a lot different.

They had caught Devlin in the saloon. They should have killed him right away, like Marvin Hurlan had ordered, but Len had wanted to question him. What Len wanted, Len got.

Len had gotten excited when Devlin had told them that McCann had a map to other gold diggings near Central City. Then Len had decided that they would wait and learn more about this by questioning the derby man's partner, only no one knew it would be this tall gunman, who could more than hold his own against anybody.

"I wish you hadn't wanted it that way, older brother," Carlton said to himself as he dug. "Things might be a lot different now. As it stands, I have to get this big gunman for you myself. But I'll do it. I swear!"

Carlton laid down the shovel and untied his brother from the horse, easing the body to the ground. He wrapped his brother in a saddle blanket and maneuvered him into the hole.

"I've got an idea, big brother. I know how to stop this Joel McCann. I'll make it work."

Carlton began filling in the grave, weeping bitterly. He couldn't remember the last time he had cried, possibly as a child, and the tears felt odd as they ran down his face.

When he had finished, he wiped his cheeks. He stood a long time in the darkness, listening to the slow trickle of the water, thinking about his plan.

It involved a gunfighter who also worked for Marvin Hurlan, a gunfighter who owed him a favor. During questioning, Devlin had said that he and his partner were going back to Colorado together, by way of Cimarron. Devlin's partner, McCann, wanted to find his wife and son, who were supposedly somewhere in the town.

Yes, McCann and Devlin would go to Cimarron and they would meet with Hank Trent. If there was anyone who could take care of McCann, it was Hank Trent.

Trent had worked for Marvin Hurlan for five years. Three years past, both Carltons had teamed up with Trent to pull off some jobs ordered by

Hurlan. Trent would have been killed during one of the jobs had it not been for Lon Carlton.

"I shot that miner before he could get his gun up," Carlton remembered telling Trent. "Lucky I was there for you."

"Lucky that you were," Trent had agreed. "I owe you one."

Carlton smiled for the first time since the shootout. "Yes, Hank Trent," he said to himself, "you owe me one. And I'm going up to Cimarron to collect."

With Marvin Hurlan's influence, Trent had gotten himself a job as a territorial marshal out of Cimarron, which made it that much easier for him to rob travelers along the Sante Fe Trail.

Trent and his partner, Chico Ruz, did a lot of thieving, splitting the take with Hurlan. Ruz, another gunman who worked for Marvin Hurlan, was a "deputy" of Trent's, someone to watch Trent's backside and be sure no one caught on to what they were doing.

Ruz was part Apache and could fight better with his eyes closed than most men could with theirs open. He and Trent both liked to use guns and knives. It would be easy to set them after McCann and Devlin.

As Carlton put a cross in place, he became eager. Nothing would please him more than to watch Trent and Ruz take care of those two.

Carlton led his horse back and forth over his brother's grave, trampling any signs of disturbance. He mounted, determined to reach Cimarron that night and find Trent and Ruz. It wouldn't be long, he believed, until he could think of this burial with peace in his mind. Maybe just a few days.

McCann slept fitfully. He had dragged a mattress from the boardinghouse into the shade of a cottonwood and had tied his horse to a limb. Devlin had pulled his shirt out and had set his red derby over his face. Loaded with whiskey, he snored like a longhorn bull.

Only when the sun fell and the wind quieted did McCann finally rest easy. A cool stillness had settled in, and a half-moon hovered in a star-shot sky.

Near midnight, McCann rose and pulled his gun. A shadow emerged from behind the boardinghouse.

"Don't shoot me. I've come to give you news."

McCann recognized the bartender's voice.

"Come ahead," McCann said, rising to his feet. "Move easy."

"I don't want no trouble," the bartender said. "I figured I'd tell you that you don't have to worry about that last gunman."

"What are you talking about?" McCann asked.

"Lon Carlton, the younger one. He's the one that got away. Late this afternoon he took his dead brother and rode out. He left DuCain behind."

"Why are you telling me this?" McCann asked. "The way you acted before, I'd think you'd want to shoot me."

"I know better than to try," the bartender said. "I just thought you'd like to know that the last of the three rode out. That's all. I could cook something for you. I've got food."

McCann studied the bartender. "Why have you turned so friendly?"

"I'll be truthful," the bartender replied. "I got a letter from my daughter a week ago. She's headed to Central City by wagon, from Cimarron. I figured since you're headed over that way, you might take something to her for me."

"What do you want me to take?"

"If you'll let me cook you something," the bartender said, "I'll tell you more. She can help you, she and her husband. It'll be worth your while."

"You can get started cooking," McCann said. "We'll be in directly."

When the bartender had left, McCann rousted Devlin, who sat up, groaning.

"Wake up," McCann said. "We'll have a bite to eat. Then we'll be on our way."

Devlin looked into the sky and mumbled something about it being too dark. He lay back down and started snoring again.

McCann shook him. "Up, Corky. Up!"

"For the love of God!" Devlin said. "Can't you leave a man in peace?"

"Do you want to go to Colorado or not? It makes no difference to me."

"We don't have to go right *now*," Devlin protested.

"Corky, we go now or you're on your own."

"No, lad. You can't mean that."

"Yes."

Devlin sat up. "You'd pass up all that gold?"

"We won't get to it lying here all night," McCann pointed out. "More important, you told me that you'd heard something about my family."

"Yes, that's true. I heard that someone who fits the description of your Minnie is a washerwoman in Cimarron."

"Are you sure?"

"The man who told me was a miner. He was headed north to Colorado. We had a drink together and he told me about this woman who had taken in his clothes. He said that she told him she wanted to go north to Colorado. This miner said she was as pretty as a picture, her face freckled and all. He said she had one blond eyebrow and one red, just like you told me. And she had a boy, nearly five years old. I figure it's got to be your Minnie."

"It would sure seem that way," McCann said. "We'll eat and be on our way."

"What's the hurry?" Devlin asked. "If she's been there for a spell, she'll likely be there a spell longer."

"Do you think I'm going to loiter around here when my wife's just up the trail? I wouldn't stop to eat, but I'm about done in. I need a good meal."

"You eat and I'll sleep until you're done."

"No, you'll eat, too. You need it just as bad."

"But my bones ache."

McCann untied his horse. "They'll ache less in the saddle than on the ground."

Devlin groaned again and stood up. "You've not changed even a little, have you, lad? Always wanting it *your* way. Never giving a man a little rest." He struggled to tuck his shirt in. "I should have never met you. I shouldn't have helped you in the army. I shouldn't have ever told you about the gold. I should have kept it for myself. All of it. I could have gotten some sleep."

"You're just too honest, Corky," McCann said. "Let's see what that bartender wants to feed us."

"I wouldn't trust him, not me," Devlin said.

"He's not as bad as he seems," McCann said. "I think he was scared, mainly, and was trying to pick the side he thought would win."

"He didn't do me no favors."

"Maybe he's trying to make up for it by offering to feed us," McCann said. "That's a nice gesture."

"Maybe," Corky said as they walked toward the boardinghouse. "But you take the first bite."

Four

Inside the boardinghouse, the bartender had fixed beef and beans, with tortillas. With unusual calmness, he served the meal to McCann and Devlin. McCann hadn't had a warm meal in over two days, and Devlin ate as if he'd hungered just as long.

"I'll tell you more about my daughter," the bartender said, seating himself. "Her name's Martha Jacobson. She's my only child, and she's got a young son. I hate to see them go up to the gold fields. It's dangerous country."

"And you're saying this is God's heaven?" Devlin asked. "I've never been treated so harshly."

"You ain't dead, are you?" the bartender asked. "If you weren't such a good liar, and your friend here so good with a gun, those killers would have hung you out to dry. Tell me I'm wrong."

Devlin shrugged and filled his mouth with food, washing it down with whiskey.

"What makes you think we can find your daughter?" McCann asked the bartender.

"I know you're headed through Cimarron," the bartender said. "Her husband was a noted lawyer there, before he headed to the gold fields. Anyone can tell you where she lives. I just want you to find her before she leaves to find him."

"What if she's already gone?" McCann suggested. "What if we have to look for her on the trail? There's bound to be a lot of women who look like her."

"Maybe, but I doubt it," the bartender said. "She's blond and taller than most women. She has a little scar just above her left eye that she got when she fell on a rock as a child. Didn't even cry. If you see her from a distance, you can tell, too. She walks like she knows who she is."

"Sounds like she's a proud woman," Devlin said. "Must have gotten it from her mother's side."

The bartender glared at Devlin. McCann cleared his throat. "Maybe she'd stand out in a crowd," he said, "but it's still a tall order."

"I don't believe in miracles," the bartender said, "but I figure you're a man who can do whatever he sets his mind to. I wouldn't ask you, but I don't see another way of reaching her." He pulled an envelope from his pocket. "If you'd give this to Martha. I thought I should write her. She doesn't know about her mother."

McCann took the note. "Are you saying that her mother passed on and you want me to get this to your daughter?"

"That's the only reason I'd trouble you," the bartender said. "My wife passed on two days back. It was sudden. I don't know what took her. Fever is all I can say. I buried her under the trees in back."

"I'm sorry to hear that," McCann said.

"Yeah, maybe I've been a wee bit harsh," Devlin added. "I shouldn't be that way."

"No, you both have the right to be angry," the bartender said. "I was putting my cards on those other men. But I should've known they'd never have helped me."

"They'd probably have killed you," Devlin suggested. "They'd have used you for what they needed, then killed you. Ah, but they were a bad lot."

The bartender shrugged. "Maybe. But I wouldn't care about dying now, except that I want Martha to get the letter. I'd like her to know about her mother. Maybe she'll come back with the boy. He's a fine child."

McCann stood up and stuffed the envelope into his pants pocket. "If we find her, I'll give her the letter. I'll do the best I can, but I can't promise anything."

"I wish you good luck in finding your own family," the bartender said. "It's hard out there, on men and women both. But women alone with children find it very hard to survive. A lot of them don't."

McCann and Devlin left the saloon. They mounted and headed into the darkness. The night was cool and the trail well lit by moonlight. The horses would move faster and need less water than by day. It was a good time to travel.

McCann was intent on reaching Cimarron and doing what he could to find his wife and son. It would be good to find the bartender's daughter, too.

But that was something he didn't think about very hard. The chances were better than even that Martha Jacobson had left Cimarron and was already in Colorado. The bartender was just wishing for something he couldn't have.

As he rode, McCann thought about what the bartender had said, about how hard it was for women and children, especially those who were without a man. In his mind he couldn't see Minnie with anyone else but him. It had been a long time since he had seen her, though, and anything was possible.

But if she wasn't with anyone, surviving on her own would be an incredible struggle. What the bartender had said about many of them not making it was all too true, and it made McCann ride all the harder.

Streaks of scarlet lined the dawn sky when they rode into Cimarron. The little town was already bustling with workers and ranchers getting an early start on the day. The night spots were dormant. Though some of the saloons were still open, the music and drinking had died down to nothing.

Nestled in a little valley at the base of the Sangre de Cristo mountains, the town had grown up around a gristmill built by land baron Lucien Maxwell. The mill had provided steady employment for a number of people, including the Navajos, whose farming practices had long ago brought prosperity to the region.

Maxwell liked gambling and had established a number of gaming rooms, as well as a large hotel and casino known as the Maxwell House.

As a major stop along the Sante Fe Trail, Cimarron had grown to host all kinds of travelers. Saloons and gaming rooms lined the street from end to end. Livery and dry goods businesses had been established to accommodate the many who were settling in the area.

But now there were rumors that Maxwell was selling his holdings to a syndicate. He wasn't in town often any more, and an air of uneasiness had settled over the town he had built nearly singlehandedly.

McCann and Devlin ordered eggs, potatoes, and beef at the Maxwell House. McCann was restive, wanting to locate every washerwoman in the town.

Cimarron was small enough that the cook knew everyone in the surrounding area. He had, indeed, seen a young woman who fit the description of McCann's wife, Minnie, and a boy who would likely be her son.

"She was in town for some time, washing clothes," the cook said. "I saw her two nights past with three men on the north end of town, getting horses shod. I don't know any more than that. I hope I've helped."

"You've been a great help," McCann said, rising. He took his hat from the rack and paid for the meal.

"One other thing," the cook said. "Maybe you could help us." He eyed McCann's pistol. "We have a marshal that comes through here who's a bad one. A marshal and a deputy."

"What do you mean?"

"I mean, you should look out. He was talking to a stranger in here last night, and I heard the stranger say something about Carminga and a buckskin horse."

Devlin looked at McCann. "What's he telling you, lad? Is there somebody here who knows you?"

"I can't think who it would be." He turned to the cook. "Are you trying to warn me about something?"

"Yes," the cook said. "Both you and your partner there. A lot is going on around here now. This marshal, Hank Trent, and his deputy, Chico Ruz, they rob and steal. Not many know this. Those who find out, they kill. The stranger was talking to them about you, and about a red derby hat."

"We'll be out of town before long," McCann said. "Just as soon as I find my wife and son."

The cook shuffled his feet. "I helped you as best I could. I was thinking that maybe you can help us."

"Like I said, I just want to find my wife and son," McCann told him. "I don't need to get mixed up in anything else."

The cook shrugged. "Just be careful."

In the street, McCann discovered a large, unshaven man inspecting his horse. With him was a smaller, dark-eyed man with a hatchet face and a thin mouth.

McCann stepped toward them and saw that they both wore badges.

"I need a word with you, mister," the bigger man said to McCann. "My name is Hank Trent. I'm the marshal of these parts. This is my deputy, Mr. Ruz."

Onlookers had begun to gather. Chico Ruz, the deputy, was standing to the side, chewing on a toothpick, eyeing McCann up and down. McCann studied him, judging him to be part Indian, likely Apache.

Though irritated, McCann knew he couldn't force the issue. A lawman had stopped him for some reason, and the people gathering would side with him.

Colorado Gold

He couldn't understand why Trent would be detaining them, though.

"I see you studying my horse," McCann said to Trent. "Is there something wrong?"

Trent grinned crookedly. He brought a knee up into the buckskin's stomach, forcing a rush of air from the horse.

"It appears your cinch was loose," Trent said, tightening the straps. "You might have fallen off."

McCann started toward Trent. "That's no way to treat a horse, mister."

"Just rest easy," Ruz said, pulling his pistol. "Now, take a step back."

McCann took a deep breath and moved back to where Devlin stood watching, his eyes narrowed.

"I don't like this a-tall," Devlin said. "Something smells like rotten eggs."

Trent turned to McCann. "I have some questions to ask you about your horse." He pointed to Devlin's horse. "And this one, also. Does it belong to your partner? That man with the red derby?"

Devlin shuffled from foot to foot. "Yes, that's my horse."

"Yep, I've got questions about these two horses," Trent repeated, looking into the saddlebags of McCann's horse.

"What questions do you have, Marshal?" McCann asked.

Trent pulled out a frying pan, returned it, and turned to McCann. "I'll ask the questions when I'm ready. You'll answer them right away. Do you understand?"

Devlin continued to shuffle from foot to foot. He eyed the deputy, Ruz, who continued to hold his pistol ready to fire.

Trent leaned against McCann's buckskin. "You say this is your horse?"

"Has been since the battle of Shiloh," McCann replied.

"Really?" Trent said, the twisted grin widening. "Which side did you fight on?"

"Does it matter now?"

Trent frowned. "It does to me."

"What's that got to do with our horses? The war's been over four years."

"Maybe that war," Trent said. "But there'll always be wars that we've got to fight. You know, against those who break the law."

McCann noticed that the people who had gathered were now staring at him as though Trent's words must be true, as though he and Devlin must be outlaws.

"We haven't broken any laws," McCann told the marshal. "Is there a reason for all this?"

"I told you I'd ask the questions," Trent snapped. "You'd best understand that."

"It's highly irregular to hold men unless you've arrested them," McCann pointed out.

"I can hold you as long as I want," Trent said. "Don't go getting impatient with me."

"Listen, I've got some folks I need to meet," McCann said. "Those horses aren't stolen, so my friend and I would like to be on our way."

Trent looked to Ruz, who came toward McCann, his pistol leveled. "I'd step back if I were you. The marshal needs to take those horses as evidence."

"Evidence of what?" McCann asked.

"These horses are stolen," Trent told McCann. "Since you just said that you and your partner rode in on them, then it must be you two who stole them."

The people gathered began to talk among themselves, some angrily.

"There's been a mistake for sure," McCann said. "We just got into town. We haven't been here an hour."

"Did you ride up from Carminga?"

"Yes. How did you know?"

"There's no mistake about it, then," Trent said. "A man came into town late last night, claiming that you stole these horses from him and his brother. He says you shot his brother, and that he barely got away. A killer and a horse thief to boot. You're in real trouble."

"Where's the man now?" McCann asked.

The marshal pointed to where Lon Carlton stood leaning against a hitching post nearby, smirking.

"I should've figured he was part of this, the snake that he is," Devlin said. "If that don't beat all."

"Are you saying that man over there is the one making the accusations?" McCann asked Trent.

"He's the very one."

"What makes you so certain what he said is true?"

"I intend to find out what's true," Trent said. "That could take some time. So, until it's settled, there's a cell big enough for both of you right down the street."

"There's no evidence against us," McCann said. "Just that man's word. What makes you want to believe him?"

"I've got a job to do," Trent said, his eyes hard.

"You can do as I say, or die in the street. It makes no difference to me."

McCann saw the intent in Trent's eyes. Make one move for his gun, and Trent would kill him. Trent wanted the excuse.

Had there not been a crowd gathered, McCann felt that Trent would have pulled the trigger with no excuse at all. But he had to make it look legitimate by taking them to jail first.

Trent called Ruz close to him. "Take the horses along to the jail. And keep the people from gathering over there."

Ruz nodded and began untying McCann's buckskin. McCann gritted his teeth. There was nothing he could do. He and Devlin would be locked up. But he vowed to himself that it wouldn't be for long.

Five

As McCann handed his gun to Trent, he saw a tall, blond woman watching from the crowd. Martha Jacobson. He looked hard for his wife and son, but they were not to be seen.

McCann felt like breaking away and running. He couldn't miss them now, not when he was so close.

Trent rammed his pistol barrel into McCann's ribs. "I said march. I haven't got all day."

With Devlin close behind, McCann walked to the jail and stepped into the cell. Out of sight of the townspeople, Trent brought his pistol down against the back of McCann's head. Ruz stood in the doorway, talking to the people in the street, getting them to disperse.

McCann slumped to the floor, groaning. Trent kicked McCann twice before Devlin stepped in.

"Are you interfering with the law?" Trent asked.

He brought his gun up to strike Devlin. A voice from the doorway stopped Trent from bringing the barrel down into Devlin's face.

"Marshal, I would like to see the prisoners please."

Martha Jacobson stood in the doorway, her expression firm. She wore a homemade split riding skirt and boots. Blond hair trailed out from under a wide-brimmed hat and down across her shoulders, framing her face and strong blue eyes.

Trent looked to Ruz, who shrugged and said, "She pushed past me."

"Did you hear me, Marshal?" the woman asked. "I want to visit the prisoners." She stepped toward the cells. "You remember me, Marshal. Martha Jacobson. My husband, Blaine, is the lawyer who works for Mr. Maxwell."

Trent was stiff with his reply. "Yes, I do remember."

"Good. I want to see the prisoners. They have a right to counsel."

Devlin had been helping McCann. "She's right!" he yelled at Trent. "The law states that we've got a right to a lawyer!"

"I'll tell you what the law says around here!" Trent said. He glared at Devlin.

"Marshal," Martha said, "you can't deny a prisoner his right to counsel. That's what the law reads."

"But you're not a lawyer."

"I'll do until my husband gets here."

"But why are you interested in these men?"

"What business is that of yours, Marshal?"

Trent stared. He realized that Maxwell had a lot of authority in the area and that Blaine Jacobson was a well-respected lawyer. He still couldn't understand why she had come in to see these two. As far as he knew, neither of these men had ever been to Cimarron.

Yet he couldn't go against this woman. If Maxwell became angry with him for some reason, there might be an investigation into his activities as a lawman. He didn't want that.

"I guess it would be all right to visit them," Trent said reluctantly. "I don't know if it's a good idea, though."

McCann came to his feet, rubbing the back of his head. The blow had been glancing, as McCann had noticed Trent's intention just in time to begin ducking. Still, he was dazed and his head ached.

"What happened to that man?" Martha asked. "He seems to have been hurt."

"He fell is all," Trent said. "I guess he's trail-weary. Why don't you come back when they've rested up."

Martha's eyes narrowed. "I'd like to see them now, if you please. I haven't got all day."

"These men are very dangerous," Trent said. "You shouldn't do this."

"I'm not worried," Martha said. "Now, if you'll excuse us."

Martha stepped between Trent and McCann, who was standing just inside the cell. The door was open, the key resting in the lock.

"You can wait outside," Martha told Trent. "I'll call you when I'm ready."

"I'm telling you, Mrs. Jacobson, you shouldn't—"

"I'll call you when I'm ready, Marshal." She stared at Trent coldly.

Trent pulled the key from the lock. "I'm not going to lock you in there with them. That would be foolish."

"I have no fear of them."

"No, no. I still figure to protect you, ma'am." The wry grin returned to Trent's mouth. He sat down in his chair and tossed the key onto his desk. "No one would fault me for that. You go ahead and talk to them, with the cell open. I'll just wait over here until you're through."

"We need privacy, Marshal."

"That's the best I can do," Trent said. "Like I said, no one would fault me for staying close, in order to protect you." He looked to Ruz, who came into the room and sat down in a chair along the wall. "That's what we're both sworn to do: uphold the law and protect the citizens."

Lon Carlton walked into the room, holding the whiskey bottles that Devlin had taken from the saloon. He set them on Trent's desk.

"They've robbed my saddlebags," Devlin said. "The snakes!" He started out of the cell. McCann held him back.

Trent opened a desk drawer and pulled out two glasses. Apparently Ruz didn't drink. He acted like he didn't even want to be around it.

Trent blew the dust from the glasses and set them on the table. Then he shoved McCann's gun belt into the drawer and closed it.

"We'll be right here if you need us, ma'am," Trent told Martha. "I can't let you stay back there long."

"I'll stay as long as I wish, Marshal," Martha said. "Maybe I should have Mr. Maxwell look into all this. You're being very difficult."

Trent had been pouring drinks for himself and Carlton. He stood up quickly. "Listen, take all the time you need. I'm just a little worried about you, that's all."

"You should be worried," Martha said, "but not about me."

McCann was at the back of the cell, looking out through the bars. In the distance the Sangre de Cristos rose majestically into the simmering summer sky. Devlin and Martha Jacobson walked over next to him.

"My name is Joel McCann," he told Martha. "My friend here is Corky Devlin."

"Pleased to know you, ma'am," Devlin said, tipping his derby. "You talk mighty strong."

"Thank you," Martha said. "A woman has to learn the art of strong speech in these parts."

Devlin was licking his lips. "I was thinking, why don't you go over there and get one of them bottles they took from me. They'd give one up if you'd talk tough like you do. I'd appreciate it, I would."

"You can get more another time," McCann said. "We need to find a way to get out of here."

"I'm hoping to help you," Martha said.

"We're both obliged," McCann said. "But I find it unusual that a woman would come to the aid of two men she doesn't know. Can you tell me, Mrs. Jacobson, how that came to be?"

"I have two reasons," Martha said. "The main one has to do with my parents. I overheard Trent asking you if you came by way of Carminga. There's only one man who runs that town, and that's my father. I was hoping you might have news of him and my mother. She's been in steadily failing health the last two years. I wrote them that I was leaving for Colorado, but I never got an answer. It's usually my mother that writes. I'm worried."

McCann reached into his pocket and pulled out the letter he had gotten from the bartender. "It so happens your father gave this to me, in hopes I would run into you here in Cimarron. Funny how things work out."

Martha took the letter. Her hands were shaking. "*He* wrote the letter? My father wrote it, not my mother?"

"Your father wrote it," McCann said. "You can read it now if you'd like. But I'll warn you, the news isn't good."

Martha took the letter and stepped away from McCann and Devlin. She already knew what to expect, but couldn't put off reading it. Tears flowed from her eyes as she read:

Carminga, NM
3 May 1869

My Dear Martha,
It is hard for me to write this. You can understand. Your mother and I were together many years and had a lot of good times together. Raising you made us both very happy.

Your mother passed on two days past. A fever took her quickly. As you know, she took ill some time back. She had wanted to see you. Maybe in heaven.

Hope this letter finds you and the boy in good health. I know nothing will keep you from going to find your husband in Colorado. If you

*decide to stay in these parts, you can come down here. It's not much, but it's home to me.
Please think about me.*

*I love you, your father,
Spencer Booth*

Martha dried her eyes and folded the envelope into a pocket of her dress. At the desk, Trent and the others were talking low.

"I feel bad that I didn't go and see them, at least once," Martha said. "Oh, for goodness' sake! Why am I telling you all this? It's nothing you care to hear. I'm sorry."

"Don't apologize," McCann said. "We've all got our family problems. I'm having a hard time staying in this cell right now. My wife was seen in town as recently as day before yesterday, getting ready to leave. I haven't seen her since before the surrender. I've been looking a long time and finally caught up with her. Then I run into this marshal."

"What does your wife look like?" Martha asked.

McCann described her. "She's apt to be with three men," he said. "And she has our son with her. He should be close to five now."

"He's my son's age," Martha said. "He's with friends who've already left for Colorado. They've been gone about three days. I'd be gone myself, but I'm waiting for a telegraph from my husband."

"Well, you've got the letter," McCann said. "How did you expect to help us?"

"I don't know," Martha said. "I really don't. But I don't intend to just leave you now."

"Maybe you can tell the people that we've done nothing wrong," Devlin suggested. He was licking his lips, staring at the men as they drank. "Get them together. Have them all come over here and free us."

"They're all afraid of Trent and his deputy," Martha said. "Trent goes around the area telling people that he's protecting them. I think he's been robbing them. There've been a lot of goods stolen, and he can't seem to catch who's doing it."

"What about your husband?" McCann asked. "How long would it take him to get down here? I can pay his price."

"When I get his wire back, I'll ask him," Martha said. "He should be able to make it in a few days at most. In the meanwhile, maybe I can find your wife and son. If they're with somebody, there may be a way for them to help, also."

"Anything's better than this," McCann said. "We can't afford to stay in here much longer."

At the table, Trent had just finished his glass. Carlton was filling his, and Ruz was standing in the doorway, nodding, listening to instructions from Trent. After a moment Ruz was gone, riding out somewhere.

Martha left the jail, walking past them, saying nothing to either of them. Trent studied her, then got up and strolled back to McCann and Devlin. He ordered them into the back of the cell and slammed the door shut. He stared at them through the bars.

"She can't do you any good."

McCann spoke quickly. "She's going to talk with Maxwell and wire her husband to come here. He should get here in the morning."

"I told you," Trent said, his crooked smile broad, "that won't do you any good. We don't have time to wait for Mrs. Jacobson or her husband. We don't want them butting in on your punishment."

McCann looked at Carlton, who was drinking and smiling, staring back into the cell. Above the desk was a rack of rifles, many different kinds. Carlton stood and pulled one down. He worked the lever and aimed into the cell at McCann. He pulled the trigger, and the hammer clicked against an empty chamber.

Trent and Carlton laughed. "Lucky you," Trent told McCann. "But before we're done, you'll wish it had been loaded. That would be easier for you."

"You can't do anything to us without a trial," Devlin said.

"You'll have a trial," Trent said. "Our trial." He laughed and looked to McCann. "Don't you figure it will be a fair trial, Mr. Big Gunman?"

McCann turned away and looked out the window.

"You don't seem too concerned, do you?" Trent said. "What's the matter? Won't you be mining your gold claim up in Colorado? Mr. Joel McCann, deceased, will no longer have a claim. Nor will his partner, Mr. Devlin." He laughed again.

McCann turned back. "That's what this is all about, huh? You must know Marvin Hurlan, then. You're with Carlton. You shouldn't be telling your connections. That's dangerous."

"I don't plan to worry about what's dangerous," Trent said. "But you should. Come evening, we'll all go for a little ride, out into the country a ways. Someplace quiet, where we won't be disturbed. We'll have our own court there. Justice will be served."

Six

Lon Carlton felt content. The whiskey was sitting good inside him, and soon he would be watching McCann and Devlin both swinging at the end of a rope.

A fitting end, Carlton thought, for the man who had gunned down his brother. It wouldn't replace Len, but it would be sweet to watch that tall gunman die.

It would happen just as soon as Ruz got back to town. He had gone to select a tree that would do for both of them. Trent had told him that usually he and Ruz just shot whoever got in their way. But this was a special occasion, and they needed a tree that would hold up to a couple of hangings.

Carlton was anxious for it to happen. He wanted it soon, before the big gunman found a way out of it. He didn't want that man anywhere near a gun again.

Colorado Gold   47

As he drank with Trent, he learned a little about the business of looting travelers. It was very profitable, especially for a territorial marshal. Just wear an old pair of clothes and a mask, take the money and goods from the travelers, and change into regular clothes and a star to talk to the victims.

Marvin Hurlan had to be happy as well. He was making money without lifting a finger. All he had to do was continue to exert his influence throughout the region, telling everyone what a good job Trent was doing as a territorial marshal.

A lot of travelers had been robbed, yet nobody had caught on yet. Carlton saw Trent as very lucky. Sooner or later all good things came to an end. The trick was to get out before the end.

It was easy to say that now, with Len dead. They could have gotten the tall gunman if they'd just had a little more patience. They shouldn't have gone back into that saloon in Carminga to surprise him. They should have known he couldn't be surprised.

Carlton fidgeted in his chair. Ruz hadn't returned yet. How long would it take to find the tree? Ruz had to go a distance off the main trail, but not too far. He should be back any time.

One more glass of whiskey, Carlton told himself. It won't hurt. Just one more. Then Ruz would be back and they could get on with the hangings.

Martha Jacobson entered the jail quietly. She was holding a Colt .44, Army model. She cocked the pistol and leveled it on Trent.

Trent jerked back in his chair. His hand went to his side.

"Easy," Martha warned. "I can use this, believe me, I can."

"What do you think you're doing?" Trent asked.

"I'll do the talking," Martha said. "You'll do the listening. Just put your hands on the desk. Palms up. Slowly."

Lon Carlton set his whiskey glass down quietly. Martha turned her pistol on him.

"You, too," she said. "Reach over and put your hands on the desk. Do it slowly."

"I'm not part of this," Carlton said.

"You're wrong," Martha said. "And if you don't do what I say, right now, you're dead wrong."

Carlton leaned over and placed his hands, palms up, on the table. Frustration mixed with the whiskey inside him. His blood was heating with anger.

He weighed the alternatives. Any way he looked at it, he couldn't shoot the woman. Nothing could justify that in the eyes of the townspeople. He would have to wait for her to make a mistake, then take her gun.

Where was Ruz? Ruz had better return quickly. So close to hanging the big gunman and this has to happen.

As he studied Martha Jacobson, Carlton realized she was too smart to make a mistake, and too cool to get worried about making one. It appeared as if the tall gunman and the derby man were having a streak of luck.

Martha took the bunch of keys from the top of the desk. "If either one of you move at all, I open fire. I don't care, I'll start shooting. If you don't believe me, just try something."

She had the keys in her hand, the barrel of her .44 just inches from Trent's face.

"There's no call for this," Trent told her. "You're breaking the law."

"You'd know about that," Martha said, backing toward the cell. "Your game of robbing and stealing in these parts is about over."

Martha extended her hand back, dangling the keys for McCann, at the same time keeping her eyes on Trent and Carlton. McCann reached through the bars and took the keys, quickly working one into the lock.

Carlton rose from his chair. He was but two steps from the door. He covered that with ease and darted out into the street, untying his horse.

Trent, his eyes wide, started to rise. Martha was there, her Colt in his face once again.

"Your friend took a calculated risk and won. You just sit still."

Outside, Carlton was riding hard through the street, yelling that the outlaws were loose in the jail.

McCann and Devlin were out of the cell. McCann's head still bothered him; but it could be worse, he thought, and concentrated on the breakaway.

While Devlin watched the door and Martha covered Trent with her pistol, McCann opened the desk drawer that held his Colt and gun belt. He strapped his gun on quickly. Devlin grabbed a bottle from atop the desk and kissed it.

McCann then reached above the desk and selected rifles for himself and the other two. He and Devlin already carried one each, but backup wouldn't hurt. Partial payment for their time and the trouble they had been caused.

He took Henry .44 repeaters for Martha and Devlin. For himself, he found a Sharps .50-caliber rifle, one of the new models that fired metallic cartridges. He couldn't have found a better gun to suit his purposes. It might be the key to whether or not they got to Colorado.

McCann handed the Henry rifles to Devlin, who took them out to the horses. "I can't say that our stay's been any pleasure," McCann told Trent. "We'll be on our way. And I wouldn't suggest following."

"You're crazy if you think you'll get out of here," Trent told McCann.

Devlin came back, and McCann handed him the Sharps. Devlin was out the door, and Martha was right behind him. McCann had never taken his eyes off Trent, who now rose from his chair, reaching for his gun.

McCann's Colt was in his hand, blazing, before Trent could pull his pistol. Three quick shots to the chest knocked him backwards and to the floor.

McCann hurried out. Devlin had tied the Sharps to McCann's saddle and had helped Martha onto Trent's horse. In the streets, people were staring, many running for cover.

Devlin held the reins to McCann's buckskin. "I figured it might come to that. Now what do we do?"

"We ride out of here," McCann said, mounting, "as hard as we can. No one will see my side of this, anyway. Let's just hope this town is slow in getting together a posse."

Lon Carlton waited in the middle of the street. The tall gunman was riding straight for him. He wanted to pull his gun, but his muscles cramped. He turned his horse and rode for a side street.

Carlton watched them leave town in a cloud of dust. He rode back toward the jail, cursing himself.

Colorado Gold

He had had the chance to shoot McCann. Maybe. He would never know.

He rode back to the jail, justifying his cowardice. It had been a bad angle. He couldn't have gotten off a clean shot. There had been three of them. He wouldn't have stood a chance.

Now the tall gunman and the derby man had gotten away. That was going to mean trouble if they got to Central City.

Carlton didn't know how he was going to keep them from getting to Central City now. They'd been right where he had wanted them, and he hadn't been able to take advantage of it.

The only possible way to stop them now was to organize a posse. But there were only a few townspeople who could do him any good. Ruz was about the only one who would care enough to ride hard after McCann and the derby man. One or two of the others might, but not many.

Where was Ruz, anyway? He should have been back a long time ago. It couldn't take that long to find a tree.

Carlton tied his horse in front of the jail. The street was crowded with chattering people. Inside the jail, a doctor was bent over Trent. He shook his head.

"He's gone. Three bullets, two through the heart. Whoever shot him was a professional."

Suddenly Ruz was there, dismounting, pushing his way through the spectators to Carlton. He said something under his breath in Apache, then something in Spanish.

"What is this?" he asked, staring at Trent's body. "What happened?" Again he muttered in Apache.

Carlton pulled him into a corner. "Where have you been?"

"You know where I've been. How did this happen?"

"That woman, Martha Jacobson, sprung them. If you'd hurried up, things would be different." Carlton's voice was hard with contempt. "We *had* them, Ruz. They were in our *laps*, just waiting to die!"

"I still don't see how it happened," Ruz said. "How did they break free?"

"Martha Jacobson left and came back with a gun," Carlton explained. "She got the drop on us. There was no way to do anything without getting shot."

"And Trent tried to stop them from escaping?" He was staring at Trent's body as they hauled him out. It didn't seem possible that someone could have killed him. He began swearing in Spanish.

"I can't understand you," Carlton said.

"I just want to know how it happened," Ruz said.

"McCann gunned him down. That's what happened. So what took you so long to find a tree and throw some ropes over the limbs?"

"Difficulties," Ruz said. Even through his Spanish accent the word was strong, as if saying, *Don't talk to me about it.*

Carlton pressed him. "What kind of complications?"

"I owe you no explanations," Ruz snapped.

Since Ruz didn't drink in the first place, he certainly hadn't stopped in any saloon. There had to be another reason he had taken so long.

"Have you got a woman you went to see?"

Ruz muttered in Spanish.

Carlton leaned forward. "What?"

Ruz glared at him. "No. No woman."

"Are you sure?"

"I said, no!"

"I'd hate to think that there was a woman," Carlton said. "Because if you spent time with a woman and didn't get back here so we could hang those two, then I would say you're to blame for what's happened here."

Ruz glared. "I don't need to take that from you. I don't even know you that well. Sure, we rode together once on a job for Marvin Hurlan, but that doesn't mean anything."

"How about Trent getting shot? Does that mean anything to you?"

Ruz turned away. "I'll go after them. I'll get them by tomorrow."

"You won't go alone," Carlton said. "We'll get a posse together."

"I don't want any posse. You can come along, if you stay out of the way and let me track. But no posse."

"There will be a posse," Carlton said. "There will be men who will want to come. That's the way it is."

"I can't travel with a posse," Ruz said.

"You'll have to get used to it," Carlton told him. "You're going to have to do what I ask of you. The people here wouldn't think highly of you if they knew there was a woman somewhere that you were seeing while Hank Trent was being gunned down."

Ruz's eyes narrowed. "What did you say?"

Carlton wished he hadn't threatened him. He could see rage in Ruz's dark eyes.

"I hope you know what's happened here," Carlton said quickly. "It's bad enough that that big gunman is loose. But the woman, too, makes it worse. She said her husband's a lawyer and that she knows what you and Trent have been doing around here. It could be hard on you."

Ruz kept glaring at Carlton. "But what did you say first, about my woman?"

So it had been a woman. Carlton was sweating and knew better than to press it. "Listen, we need to head out after them. You go for the supplies. I'll get men and offer them money. There's some gathered out in front already. We'll get started."

"I still don't like the idea of a posse. I work better alone."

"You'd better realize that we need all the men we can get," Carlton said. "If they get away, we've got serious trouble. Marvin Hurlan will be mad as hell, and that woman's husband will be investigating you. You don't want that."

"No, I don't want that," Ruz agreed. "You get the posse and I'll get the supplies. I don't like it, though, and I know there'll be trouble." His eyes were narrowed again. "When it comes, I'm going to hold you responsible."

Seven

McCann led the way toward Colorado, a hard two days' ride to the north. Water was scarce and McCann didn't know the country at all, just that the Vermejo River was thirty miles over rough, brushy country and then across a treacherous canyon now filled with summer heat.

During a stop to rest the horses, Martha Jacobson explained to him how she had come by the courage to face Trent and Carlton in the jail.

"I learned that your wife and son left town yesterday morning, headed north," she said. "I knew there would be no chance for you to catch them or even see them if you didn't get out of jail right away. In fact, the more I thought about it, the more I realized those men would kill you as soon as they could."

Martha had carried the pistol in her saddlebag, in

case of emergencies. This had been such an emergency.

"I took a chance," she said. "I know how it feels not having my son with me, and he's just up the trail. I'll see him soon. The idea that you might never see your wife and son made me take action."

"I owe you a lot," McCann said. "I aim to repay you for the kindness someday, when we get out of this mess we're in."

As they mounted, Martha pointed behind them to where a dust cloud was rising. "They've come after us. Do you figure we're going to be caught?"

"They'll have a hard time getting us," McCann said. "They'll have to work harder than they want to."

"Don't you worry your pretty little self," Devlin told Martha. "Knowing the way McCann does things, strong lad that he is, that posse's in for more trouble than we are."

Devlin knew McCann's past very well. He knew the posse would have a very hard time; as a young man, McCann had lived with the Cheyenne and had learned a great deal about surviving and living off the land.

Devlin remembered having had close calls before, during the war, when he and McCann had faced some incredible odds. If there was a man to make a stand with, it was Joel McCann.

"With Joel leading us, we'll put the slip on them pretty fast, we will," Devlin continued. "And if they keep coming, they won't go back."

"I'm glad for the confidence, Corky," McCann said. "But it won't be easy, especially with the younger Carlton wanting revenge for his older brother."

"I know you've got a few Indian tricks that will spoil their picnic," Devlin said. "And I'm ready to back you."

"I'll do what I can as well," Martha offered. "But I don't know how much help I can be."

"We'll all do fine," McCann said. "Corky's been with me during times like this. There's a lot of natural food out here to keep us going. We'll give that posse more than it can handle."

Devlin helped Martha onto her horse. "He's not telling you the half of it. He learned a bunch about fighting from the Indians. That posse's in for a surprise, it is."

As one of three boys taken from a wagon train, McCann had been given the choice either to die or learn the ways of the Plains Indian. The Cheyenne had kept him and the two other boys for nearly two years. He had been thirteen when he had been captured, and he had felt as if he were thirty when he had been traded to the Oglala Sioux.

McCann thought back on those days only rarely now. He had learned a great deal and had survived a hard life, but there was no use dwelling on things and wishing for something else. Nothing could be changed at this point.

In some ways, he felt gratitude to the Cheyenne. Though they had killed his parents and those of the other two boys, they had shown him a different way of life. They had shown him what living in touch with the land was really about. If they hadn't pushed him so hard to learn the skills of a warrior, he might have died many times since.

"It's good that you know a lot about Indian ways," Martha told McCann. "You'll need to use everything you know. Chico Ruz, Trent's deputy, is part Apache."

"I knew he had Apache in him," McCann said. "That will make it hard for us. He likely knows this country inside and out, as well."

"He knows it better than that," Martha said. "He's Jicarilla. His family lived and fought all through the Sangre de Cristos. There isn't a trail we can take that he hasn't been on."

"Then it won't do to try and fool him," McCann said.

"I doubt it will do any good at all," Martha agreed.

"I'm still not worried, not a bit," Devlin said. "I've not yet met the man the equal of Joel McCann. Ruz might be good, but I don't think he'll match up."

The heat rose and McCann's head throbbed. There were many times when he wished they could stop, but there was no possible way. They had to travel as fast as the horses could safely carry them.

As McCann led Martha and Devlin toward the canyon, he made another decision. He couldn't pull the usual tricks that might get them away from most posses. Ruz would know the tricks. Now he decided that trying to outrun the posse would be a bad idea as well.

No doubt each man would be leading a fresh horse. And Ruz would have made certain they all had good horses. In traditional Indian fashion, they could switch horses with ease, enabling them to keep up a strong pace.

Lon Carlton, if he had worked in his profession for very long, would also know this. He would understand how important it was to have a good horse that could speed you out of danger. It meant the difference between life and death.

It was very likely that Carlton had many skills himself. McCann had seen Carlton sitting his horse as they had broken from jail and ridden out of town earlier. He had believed fully that Carlton would make a stand there in the street.

But Carlton had pulled out and taken cover down a side street. That had told McCann a lot about Carlton. He would never take a chance he didn't have to, and he would have everyone else do as much of the dirty work as he could get them to do.

Carlton would likely try and get Ruz to do the dangerous work. Corky had been right: Lon Carlton was a man who would shoot you in the back.

So there could be no racing the posse. No, it would be better to ride as hard as the horses could stand and not try to cross the canyon. With tired horses on dangerous trails, there would likely be some bad falls.

Instead, they would follow the canyon until it leveled off down to the river, then cross and ride into the Raton Mountains, where the rocks and dense timber would serve as allies.

In the mountains, McCann would test Ruz and see just how much he knew. Once in cover, he could take twisting, zigzag patterns that would make no sense to anyone not familiar with guerilla warfare.

Ruz would know about this, and if he was smart, he would slow the posse down. He would wish he were on his own, so that he didn't have to wait for a number of inexperienced men. He and Carlton would wonder what was just ahead. Maybe then they would feel like the hunted, rather than the hunter.

* * *

The posse numbered seven men, counting Carlton and Ruz. Four of them were cowhands on their way to Texas who had offered to ride for the money, and one was a shopkeeper named Ivan Lenke, who was convinced he was protecting his family and property.

Carlton had told Ruz to swear each of them in as a deputy. Ruz had refused. "I told you I don't want them along," he had said. "And I'm not going to make them the law."

Carlton couldn't do the swearing in, so he dropped it. None of the five hired on had even asked about being deputized, or even seemed to care. Seven fifty a man, per day, is what Carlton had promised. He had told them they'd get paid immediately after they caught McCann and the other two, and hanged them.

The idea of getting paid right away was what had brought the cowhands along. Then they could leave immediately for Texas.

Ruz still hadn't accepted the idea. Before leaving, he had again tried to convince Carlton that just the two of them should go alone. Extra men, especially men not used to being shot at, could cause a lot more problems than they solved.

Carlton had pointed out that it was important for there to be a large posse. Everyone in the general area needed to know that there was a manhunt on and that justice was being served. It was hard to impress upon Ruz that image was very important, more important in this case than practicality.

And it had been Carlton who had insisted that each man in the posse have an extra horse. "Better to take a little more time now," he had told Ruz.

"Not everyone has an Indian pony like you do. We'll make the time up easy later, when their horses begin to wear down."

Ruz had argued that there was a lot of country to make up and that only his pony could make up the time. Maybe he should go by himself.

"I know you're used to going after people alone," Carlton had told him, "but this is different. McCann won't go down easy. You can see that already. We'll need everyone we've got."

Ruz hated working with others. Too slow. Too many mistakes. No one could keep up the pace he could, and no one could survive on as little food and water.

Besides, he knew the mountains. He knew where the trails led from the moment he got on them. There wasn't a one he hadn't been on many times. He had lived in the wild during the last free days of the Apache nation.

He could remember, as a child, running with his relatives from dragoons led by the famous scout Kit Carson. They had crossed and recrossed the mountains, hiding along rocky, timbered mountainsides and in steep, brushy canyons.

He had learned how to survive and how to get away from pursuers. With the army after them, they had separated into many smaller groups, the only way to outmaneuver the soldiers. It hadn't been enough. In the end, many of them had died, even his mother, who had been waving an American flag when she was killed.

Chico Ruz was a man without a people. Neither the Mexicans nor the Apaches wanted him, and the whites loathed him. But in Hank Trent he had found a white man who didn't care if he was a mixed blood. Hank Trent had been a man who hated everyone else as much as he did. In Hank Trent he had found a man who could kill without blinking an eye.

But now Trent was dead, at the hands of a tall gunman named McCann, who would be hard to stop. In the end, Ruz promised himself, McCann would die for taking away his only friend.

Ruz muttered to himself often. Carlton had insisted on making it hard, with his posse of cowpunchers and a soft shopkeeper. Ruz had argued with Carlton that too many men would play into the hands of McCann, keeping them from getting him.

"We can't be dragging along with all these men," Ruz had argued. "McCann will get too far ahead of us."

"We don't care how long it takes us to catch them," Carlton had told him. "It's going to be hard going for them as well as us. We just want to wear them down. That's the point. Besides, we can chase them clear up into Colorado if we have to."

But Ruz wouldn't settle down. He knew that a foe like McCann would be harder to catch with a number of people.

"We can go as far as we need to," Carlton had continued. "Clear to Denver if we have to. Since he shot Trent, it's a federal matter now."

Ruz didn't care what kind of politics it involved. McCann and the other two couldn't get away. Carlton was right: He had to stop them, or someone might learn about the robberies and murders he had committed for Trent.

Trent had always covered for him. If anything went wrong, Trent made it look good. Now there was no Trent, and Ruz worried that no one would see it his way. In fact, he knew no one would see it his way. Any excuse to hang an Indian. He had to kill McCann.

Ruz had always championed himself on his tracking abilities, so finding this gunman and the other two didn't worry him. He had found a lot of people who had gotten away from Trent and would have told authorities if they hadn't been stopped. He had tracked them down and had snuck up on them.

A knife was good for that kind of thing, something Ruz was good at and proud of.

What did bother him was knowing that McCann wasn't an ordinary gunman. Anyone who could beat Hank Trent had to be very good.

In addition, McCann knew his guns. He had picked the new Sharps rifle because he knew shooting at a distance would be to his advantage. And a Sharps could bring a man down cleanly from nearly a mile away.

Seven men could be seen much more easily than just one or two. Ruz muttered and shook his head. The way it was looking, the chase for Joel McCann was going to be a hard one.

Eight

McCann looked over the canyon wall, down into rock and brush and scattered timber that twisted its way through the broken land toward the Sangre de Cristos. He knew that, to the east, the canyon would eventually level out and join with the Vermejo River.

But he didn't know how far that was. He only knew that they had to keep riding until they reached the Raton Mountains.

The horses were hot and smelled the water below. Often they had to hold the horses from taking deer and bighorn sheep trails down the steep sides. McCann knew that once in the bottom, they could never climb back out. They would be trapped and at the mercy of Carlton and Ruz.

Martha rode behind McCann, and Devlin brought up the rear. Martha turned and studied the country behind them often, while it appeared that Devlin was dozing in the saddle.

Devlin had tied a whiskey bottle, long since empty, to his saddle horn. He contended that a bottle, however empty it might be, was better than no bottle at all.

Martha couldn't understand why McCann and Devlin seemed unconcerned about their situation. It was too hot to feel hunger, but thirst was beginning to make her feel sick and dizzy.

Finally, when she thought she'd fall from the saddle, the canyon walls disappeared and the Vermejo River lay just ahead, across a brushy flat filled with cholla cactus.

It was a fight to keep the horses from running, and more of a fight to keep them from drinking too much. They wanted to drink their fill, but McCann knew that could kill them.

After taking in a little water, they rode for a short distance and allowed the horses to drink again. After doing this four times, the horses seemed satisfied, and they hadn't bloated themselves.

After the fourth stop, they filled their canteens and McCann set to taking cholla cactus thorns from his buckskin's legs.

"They'll stiffen up if we don't tend to them now," McCann said. "After the spines are out, rub some mud on the sores. That will help."

In some cases, little chunks of the cactus had broken off, embedding many little bristles in the horses. It took time to pull them free.

Martha didn't like the work any better than her horse did. But she realized that there was no choice.

"How much more of this country do we have?"

she asked McCann. "Are we going to be pulling cactus from our horses the whole time?"

"I've never crossed here," McCann said. "I don't think many folks come this way unless someone's chasing them. But we should be out of the cactus once we get into the mountains."

Late in the afternoon, McCann stopped again to let the horses drink and graze. They were starting up into the foothills of the Raton Mountains, through draws filled with oak and piñon pine. Soon the slopes would be fully wooded and they would be continually in cover.

"I think we've made the hardest part of this, as far as the country goes," McCann told the other two. "The mountains will be rougher going, but the cactus is gone and there'll be grass and water. And the posse won't have open country to chase us through. They might know the country better, but we'll have the upper hand."

"How can you say that?" Martha asked. "You've admitted that you don't know this country. How can we get the best of them?"

"Patience," McCann said. "We've got to go north. If they want to get us, they have to take the trails we do. Otherwise they'll lose us. That means that they can't try and second-guess us."

"How far back are they, lad?" Devlin asked. Besides his canteen, he had filled his whiskey bottle with water and was chugging on it.

McCann studied the vast country behind them. The late afternoon sun was a ball of fire in the sky, and the air shimmered with heat.

"I can't see anything now," McCann said. "They could be right behind us for all I know. Probably not. But I can't get a good look across the country until dawn, when the air's cooled down."

"Then this might be a good place to stop for a while," Martha suggested.

"We can't stop until we've gotten deep into the mountains," McCann said. "There's no doubt the posse will be going just as hard. They can't afford to stop, either."

"What about the horses?" Martha asked. "They can't keep up this pace much longer."

"There'll be grass in the mountains," McCann said. "You're right, the horses have to eat and drink. Otherwise, we'll be walking. We've got good horses, though, horses used to this kind of travel. They don't like it; but with a little rest now and then, they won't break down."

"I've already broken down," Martha said. "I don't know how much of this heat I can take."

McCann pulled a piece of plant root from his pocket. "Chew on this. It'll help. And as you're chewing, think that you can make it. Believe it. Believe that we can all make it. Think that we have to. Think of the alternative if we don't."

Chico Ruz studied the ground. The tracks were fresh, and very clear, following a trail along the canyon wall. He looked across the canyon, into the vastness of brush and rock, deciding that Joel McCann was a much smarter man than he had hoped.

He knew beyond a doubt now that McCann would not try and cross the canyon. He knew that McCann would not push tired horses and run himself into a dead end. He had played it smart and was headed for the mountains.

"What is it?" Carlton asked. "Where did they go down into the canyon?"

"They didn't go down into the canyon," Ruz said. He pointed east. "They're moving along the top, to where the canyon hits the Raton Mountains."

"But that's putting more distance between them and Colorado," Carlton said. "Why didn't they cross the canyon?"

"Maybe he doesn't know the country," Ruz said. "But he knows what he's doing. He was smart not to try and cross."

"How's that?" Carlton asked.

"We're changing horses, back and forth, all the time," Ruz said. "They've got but one horse each. Think about how hard it would be to take the horses we have across right now. We've been riding two, and still they're tired and thirsty."

"I see what you mean," Carlton said. "That's a rough trail going down there. A fall could cost them everything."

"Even if their horses were fresh, it would be hard for someone who didn't know the country," Ruz said. "McCann is smart. He won't take a chance at getting trapped. It's easy to do if you don't know the canyon."

"He's not going to be easy to catch, is he?" Carlton said. "Did you know what he was going to do?"

"He's never tried to fool us," Ruz told Carlton. "In fact, I think he's making it easy for us. He'll probably challenge us once he gets into the mountains. And that's not going to be good, not with these men."

Carlton looked back at the rest of the posse. They had all drained their canteens long ago and were talking about riding down into the canyon for water.

One of them, a tall, blond cowhand named Will Davis, was set to lead the way.

"Stop, there!" Carlton yelled. "Where do you think you're going?"

"The water's down there," Davis snapped. "Not up here."

"We don't any of us go into the canyon," Carlton said. "It's a long ways down and the horses won't want to come back out. It'll take a lot of time that we don't have."

"We can't go much farther without water," Davis said. "It's crazy to think that we can."

One of the others, another cowhand named Ike Jones, spoke up. "Why don't we cross the canyon here? We can water the horses and go on ahead. It doesn't matter that they didn't cross here. In fact, it's good for us. Maybe we can cut them off."

"Are you a tracker, Jones?" Carlton asked.

Jones, who was Davis's cousin, frowned. "No, I'm not."

"We follow Ruz, and he wants to stay with the tracks," Carlton said. "That's the way it is."

"We'd better find water quick," Davis said. "I didn't hire on to die of thirst."

Ruz spoke with contempt. "What's the matter with you, cowpuncher? We're following a woman, and she didn't have to go down there for water." He pointed into the east, toward the mountains. "She's out there somewhere, and I'll bet she's not crying around like some baby. Are you telling me that you can't keep up with a woman?"

Davis said, "She's no stronger than me, or even you. I don't care if you're Indian, you need water like everyone else. How do you know they didn't travel along the top for a ways and go down somewhere up ahead?"

"Okay, strong cowpuncher, maybe you'd like to bet on it," Ruz challenged.

Davis straightened up in the saddle. "What do you want to bet? Say, fifty dollars? Can you afford that?"

"Fifty dollars?" Ruz said. "I think I can afford that. But let's make it more."

"What do you want?" Davis asked. "How much more? You want to bet a hundred dollars?"

"No," Ruz said, "let's do it this way. If I win, I get to shoot three of your fingers off. If you win, you can shoot three of mine off. What do you say?"

Davis stared.

"I didn't hear you, cowpuncher," Ruz said. "Is that a fair bet?"

"That's crazy, Ruz," Davis said. "What's wrong with a hundred dollars?"

Ruz nodded. "Okay, let's bet a hundred dollars, and the fingers to boot. That will make it better. The man who wins can spend the money and be happy, because he knows the other man can't hold a gold piece in his fingers." He was smiling.

"I'll go for the money," Davis said. "Not the fingers."

"What's the matter, cowpuncher?" Ruz asked. "Don't you believe in yourself?"

"Money's one thing," Davis said. "And a hundred dollars is a lot. But the fingers, well, that's something I want no part of."

"Then here's what I am going to do," Ruz said. "We'll forget about the bet. How's that? But you'd better do what I say from here on or I'll shoot your fingers off anyway. Do you understand?"

Davis turned red.

"I asked you if you understood, cowpuncher," Ruz pressed.

"I understand you, Ruz." Davis was licking his dry lips. "I want you to know, I think you're crazy."

Ruz smiled crookedly. He looked at Cal and Clint Ritter, two cowhands who were brothers, neither over twenty years old. Davis and Jones referred to them as the Ritter boys.

"Okay," Ruz said, "if you want to keep your fingers, I'll shoot the fingers off the two boys. How does that sound?"

The Ritter boys lowered their heads and looked over at Davis.

"You're crazy, Ruz," Davis repeated.

Ruz kept the crooked smile. "Do you think I care how you feel about me? You all know that I don't care to have any of you along. I'd rather do it alone. But Carlton here believes there should be a lot of us. He thinks the people back in Cimarron like that. I don't know. We'll see."

Ivan Lenke, the shopkeeper, was just past forty and, as a rule, spoke very little. After hearing Ruz talk about shooting the fingers off his own posse, Lenke had begun to wonder if he should have even signed on.

But Lenke was not one to quit. He had started something and he intended to see it through. The only trouble he wanted was when they caught McCann and the other two.

With everyone staring, Ruz urged his pony ahead, following the tracks again, muttering to himself. Davis asked Carlton why he didn't say something.

Carlton shrugged, trying to hide a smile. "What did you want me to say?"

"You could have at least said something when he talked about shooting everyone's fingers off."

"That's something he'd do," Carlton said. "He wants everyone to work as hard as he is at catching McCann. He doesn't think you're working very hard at it."

"What does he want?" Davis asked. "We're riding as hard as he is. What are you saying?"

"He's the tracker," Carlton said. "His job gets harder when we don't follow him. We can't go off on our own. You've got to understand that."

"These horses are going crazy without water," Davis argued. "We can't catch anybody with horses ready to go down."

"Ruz knows horses better than you do," Carlton said. "He knows if they're ready to go down or not. He won't let that happen. Besides, he knows this country inside and out. We'll find water soon enough."

"I knew Ruz was a hard one," Davis said, "but I didn't know it would come to this."

"He's getting ahead of us," Carlton said. "We'll all stick this out together, and we'll all know we've done a good deed for Cimarron and for the territory of New Mexico."

Carlton started out with the posse behind him. Ruz was not far ahead, off his horse, studying the tracks and the country leading into the mountains.

Behind, Carlton could hear Davis talking with the others. His voice was hard. Carlton hoped that Ruz could lead them to McCann and the others before another full day went by. If they couldn't get it done by then, Carlton knew, there was going to be some real trouble.

Nine

McCann had brought them as far as they could go. To push the horses any farther would mean killing them.

The small fire crackled softly. Just enough blaze for warmth and a good meal. Nestled deep in the rocks and timber, they had no worry that the light could be seen anywhere.

They were near the headwaters of Timpas Creek, a series of boggy streams and springs where the water was sweet and cool. They had traveled hard, well into the night, leaving them less than a full day to Raton Pass.

No matter the unfamiliar ground, Martha was thankful for the rest. She had never been pushed so hard in her life. It had taken her to a new height of endurance, a level she hadn't realized she could reach.

She licked her fingers, savoring the last taste of a grouse that McCann had killed with a rock. In the Indian tradition, he had thanked the Creator for the food and also the spirit of the grouse, who had given its life to sustain theirs.

Martha had looked on with fascination. Though she had seen numerous Indians working at the gristmill in Cimarron, she was not familiar with their spiritual lives. They were quite guarded. They came to work and talked among themselves, then went home, after very little interaction with white people.

In watching McCann's solemn gratitude for the food, she realized that she had taken a lot for granted throughout her life. "We don't realize that the water we drink and the food we eat is a gift from the Creator," McCann had told her. "I learned the meaning of that while living with the Cheyenne. The whites can say all they want about Indians, but those people revere life far deeper than we do."

Devlin, on the other hand, was used to McCann. Nothing McCann might do surprised him. Though he knew little about Indian ways, he respected McCann's devotion to what he had learned from the Cheyenne.

"He's an uncommon lad," he had told Martha. "Too bad he doesn't like whiskey better. We'd have a couple of bottles for the trail, we would. But in time."

Now, in the last glow of evening, McCann hobbled the horses and left them to graze in a small meadow. He sat quietly at the top of a knoll and listened to the late evening sounds. He wanted to be certain that everything was settled and that the posse was nowhere near.

He suspected that Carlton or Ruz would be pushing the men hard. They would be traveling for as long as Ruz could make out tracks. And they would be up before first light.

As McCann didn't know the country, he had stuck to a main trail that led them toward the high country. He could tell by the old sign that the Apache had used the trail for many years. No doubt Ruz knew right where it led.

But there couldn't be any more travel, not for a while. The horses needed rest. So did everyone else. All McCann could hope for was that the posse was as tired as they were.

On the knoll, McCann continued to listen to the night sounds. There was little difference between this country and the northern mountains. Well, just the trees and grass and brush, which were all different because of the longer growing season and the hotter summer months.

But the ground was the same, the Earth Mother, as the Cheyenne had taught him. Everything was a part of the whole, everything one. If you listened correctly, the life around you would talk to you, no matter who you were.

Bone-tired and his head throbbing, McCann could do little more than stay awake. His concentration was lost for the time being. He needed sleep, and badly.

Near the fire, Martha and Devlin peered into the flames. Though pursued closely by men who wished to kill her, Martha seemed relaxed and without worry.

Possibly it was her extreme exhaustion, she told herself. Never before had she been so tired. But despite her weariness, she felt an odd sense of peace.

"It's been a while since I've spent time in the mountains," she told Devlin. "It's refreshing."

Devlin sucked water from his whiskey bottle. "Refreshing? I'll tell you, pretty lady, there are those not far behind who'd like to keep you from your comfort. Refreshed is something I am not."

"We'll make it," Martha said. "I have a lot of life left to live and I intend to see it through. I have a family that awaits me in Colorado. Life is going to be good."

"I'm thankful you sprung us from that jail, I am," Devlin said. "But it might have cost you, you see, for you don't know about your husband yet. You don't know what he's doing. You can't get a wire from him up here."

"I'm gaining some peace of mind up here," Martha said. "That helps me deal with the problems I may have to contend with later down below."

"Maybe you're a wee bit tired," Devlin suggested. "Maybe your mind is being pushed a little hard. Do you suppose?"

"I'm not going to help myself by worrying," Martha said. "I think I could do better by trying to train my mind on the positive. Maybe you should do the same, Mr. Devlin."

"I expect you're right," Devlin said. He sighed, staring at the whiskey bottle. "I don't have any of my own comfort left. I guess I'll turn in for the night."

Devlin walked a short distance away and laid out his bed roll. He stretched out, using his saddle as a pillow, and was soon snoring.

McCann came in and sat down next to Martha. "Are things all right between you and Corky?" he asked.

"Mr. Devlin is a nice man," she told McCann. "But he seems so troubled."

"He's been through a lot," McCann said. "He won't talk about it, but he's lost a lot of family, either to the war or to sickness. He might be the only one left."

"Didn't he every marry?" Martha asked.

"Once. He lost his wife and a baby girl in a wagon accident. They were crossing the Platte River, on their way to Colorado. The river was high and the wagon broke apart. He never found their bodies."

"That's horrible," Martha said. "It's a wonder he has anything to look forward to."

"I think gold is the only thing that motivates him anymore," McCann said. "And he's told me many times that he doesn't know what he'll do when the claim comes in. Wealth doesn't matter to him, either."

"He thinks a lot of you," Martha said.

"We went through the war together," McCann said. "He saved my life more than once. Since that time, we've been taking turns helping one another out of tight scrapes."

"And you both went into the Colorado gold fields together after the war?"

"We had high hopes," McCann said. "We were both running from the past. We filed our claim, gathered a few nuggets and a little dust, but didn't get much for our efforts."

"So why are you going back?"

McCann explained what Devlin had told him about a new mining process that could extract gold from rock brought up from underground.

"This railroad mogul, Marvin Hurlan, has either

bought up or stolen most of the claims in the area," McCann said. "We want to hold on to our claim, and he wants it bad."

"It sounds like your claim is a good one. But is it worth dying for?"

"It's the principle of the thing," McCann explained. "No matter if it's a big claim or a little claim that's worthless, I don't like having someone try to take what's rightfully mine. There are too many greedy big-money men who think it's their right to run over anyone they choose. I don't agree."

"So Carlton was sent by this Marvin Hurlan to get rid of you. And he just happened to know Trent and Ruz. Is that what's going on?"

McCann explained what had happened at Carminga. There had been no way of knowing that anyone had been waiting for him.

"You know the rest," McCann said. "Now Carlton has turned it around, and the law is on his side."

"You've got some heavy odds against you now," Martha said. "Killing Hank Trent has made you an outlaw, no matter that Trent was truly the offender."

"I didn't have a choice," McCann said. "I can see now that Carlton came into town ahead of us and set it all up. He must have known Carlton from before. Likely they worked together somewhere, probably robbing and killing. You seem to know a lot about Trent."

"My husband, Blaine, works for Lucien Maxwell, the man that some say started Cimarron," Martha said. "He's done a lot of Maxwell's legal work for the past four years. During that time, Trent got the job as territorial marshal. Blaine has been gathering evidence to show that Trent has been taking advantage of his position. He's been wanting to bring Trent down for some time."

"What happened that he didn't see it through?"

"He didn't think Maxwell would back him," Martha replied. "It looks like Maxwell will soon be selling out his interests around Cimarron. Without Maxwell's influence, Blaine thought he would have a hard time getting Trent indicted for his crimes."

"So your husband thought it was better to try and start over elsewhere?"

"Yes, that's about it. With Maxwell's blessing, he decided to take some time off and see what he could do in the gold fields of Colorado."

"And he left you behind?"

"It was my choice. I didn't want our young son subjected to the terrible life of a mining camp. I had made some good friends in Cimarron. Actually, they're the friends who I've decided to travel to Colorado with. I told Blaine to find what he was looking for, or get it out of his system, whichever came first, and then come back for us. If he found what he wanted and could guarantee a good life for us, then I'd go up to meet him."

"But you don't know what he's found yet, do you?"

"No, I don't. Not for certain. He wrote me two weeks ago, saying he'd filed on a claim that he knew would bring a good profit. I haven't heard from him since. I wired him and expected an answer, but now I can't stay around Cimarron to see if he's wired back."

"You'll know soon enough," McCann said. "When you catch up with your friends, you'll be about a week from Denver. Central City is just above Denver, in the mountains. Maybe there's a chance that Corky and I can help you find him, since you've done so much for us."

"I would certainly appreciate it," Martha said. "That would be very kind of you."

"It's the least I can do."

Martha looked into McCann's eyes. She wanted to lean over and hug him, to know what it felt like to hold him close, but she stopped herself.

McCann rose to his feet. "I'd better check the horses one last time before we turn in."

"I'll see you in the morning, then," Martha said.

McCann nodded. "We'll get an early start. You sleep well."

Martha smiled. "I will, thank you."

McCann watched her lay out her bedroll, then turned to check the horses. Martha was a very pretty woman, strong and pretty. Her husband was lucky to have her. He wondered how his own wife was doing and if she was on the trail somewhere just ahead; and who she was with; and if he would ever find her; and if he did, whether she would be glad to see him or not.

There were too many questions. Just too many.

Ten

Carlton sat against a tree just out from camp. The mountain night was cool and filled with soft sounds. They were of little comfort. He hadn't been able to sleep and wouldn't sleep until they got Joel McCann.

They had crossed the Vermejo River in late afternoon and had ridden on through late evening until reaching the mountains. They had lost precious time at the river as two of the men, the cowhand Davis being one of them, had overwatered their horses. Those horses had had to be left behind.

And it had taken some time to pick cholla cactus from the horses' legs. Ruz had a slick way of doing it, using mud and some kind of plant juices, but he hadn't been in the mood to help anyone else.

There were other problems that Carlton knew would grow as the chase continued. While riding toward the mountains, Carlton had insisted that they stop to scan the foothills ahead. Carlton had searched with his spyglass for any sign of McCann and the others. Ruz had become irritated and had wanted to go ahead, bringing on disruptive arguments.

"We don't need any spyglass where they're headed," Ruz had said. "McCann is no doubt in the timber by now. How do you expect to see him there? We've got their trail. I say we just keep riding."

"Did you ever think that maybe we could get an idea where they're going and cut them off?" Carlton had suggested. "Don't you want to end this soon?"

"It won't end soon," Ruz insisted. "Not the way things are going now."

"Listen," Carlton had finally told him, "you might be a tracker, but I can see a long ways. If I know where they are all the time, I feel better."

"Don't start feeling better until they're all dead," Ruz had warned. "The way it's beginning to look, we'll be having a hard time with this man. And having this posse with us will only make it worse."

Maybe Ruz had been right: Maybe just the two of them should have come alone, without a posse. They would certainly have saved a lot of time, and there would have been less friction to contend with.

Still, the townspeople would have thought it odd had just he and Ruz left to catch McCann and the other two. Always one for appearances, Carlton had insisted that the ordinary steps be taken. He had learned this from Marvin Hurlan, the railroad tycoon, who always covered his tracks and always made the right impression.

"Once you get the people to believe you," Hurlan

had said, "it's hard to get them to change their minds about you. Always make them think you're doing the right thing. The rest will fall into place."

Carlton knew they couldn't have gone alone, anyway. Davis and the other cowhands had smelled money and had insisted on going. They were just passing through on their way to Texas, to hire on one of the new cattle drives to the Kansas railheads. They needed some money to get them to San Antonio.

As it stood now, Ruz was ready to kill Davis and the others, just to be rid of them. Davis was a cowhand and not a gunman, but he was near the end of his rope. It would only be a matter of time until the shooting started, and they wouldn't be shooting at McCann.

Carlton could also see Ruz's side. Ruz was desperate. He had a lot to lose if McCann gave his testimony to another federal officer. The testimony would also involve Marvin Hurlan, if an investigation went that far. That couldn't happen.

Carlton also realized that Hurlan would blame him, personally, for the whole mess. Hurlan was expecting McCann and Devlin to be dead now. He wouldn't want to hear any excuses why things weren't the way he wanted them.

But none of it seemed that important to Carlton now. Not even Hurlan crossed his mind that often. The reason he couldn't sleep was that he kept seeing himself loading his brother's body across the saddle and burying him in a small arroyo he would likely never go back to.

There had been no other way he could have taken care of his brother. Now he would feel bad the rest of his life. It was true, Len could never come back, but McCann's death would make it easier to live with.

Davis sat next to the fire, addressing the posse members in a quiet tone. Carlton and Ruz were both gone from camp, and no one knew where they were.

Davis had returned from checking the horses to find the two absent. This had prompted him to call the meeting. The fire was down to coals and the men all leaned forward to hear.

"I don't know where those two went, but you can bet that it's not good for us," Davis was saying. "I'd say Ruz was planning something."

Jones, Davis's cousin, had been growing more nervous about the situation. He hadn't trusted Ruz from the beginning and hadn't wanted to join the posse. But Davis had convinced him that they all needed the money.

The Ritter boys had pushed cattle north with Davis before. They had found Davis to be loyal and trustworthy, and were willing to do anything he asked.

During the ride from Cimarron, they had both been content to just listen. As the matter of Ruz and Carlton became worse, they felt even more compelled to say nothing and side with Davis and Jones on anything they suggested.

Clint, the oldest, spoke up. "We started this chase with the understanding that we'd all be treated fair. When Ruz made fun of Cal and me, I knew he didn't care about any of us. I'll do what's needed to rid ourselves of him, if it comes to that."

Davis nodded. "You're two good boys. Don't you worry none. We'll come out of this just fine."

Jones brought the subject back to the absence of

Ruz and Carlton. "They wouldn't leave without us. Not now, do you think? They couldn't get that gunman McCann by themselves."

"I don't know where they went or why," Davis said. "But they went on foot. All the horses were there. I don't know why Ruz left them. You'd think he would be smarter than that, the way he cares about that pony of his."

"I think he's too crazy to know what he's doing," Jones said. "We shouldn't have come."

"There's no call to complain about coming," Davis said. "We just have to figure out a way to handle Ruz."

"Mr. Ruz is a very dangerous man, I think." Ivan Lenke had spoken rarely during the chase, but he, too, had grown more and more concerned. "He might do anything. So we must remain calm around him."

"Remain calm?" Jones said. "He'd shoot a man in his sleep. You can't be much calmer than that."

"On the other hand," Davis said, "Carlton hasn't got the spine to shoot a man in his sleep. He's afraid he would miss. But he's got Ruz to fight his battles for him."

"I still don't understand all I know about Carlton," Jones said. "What was all this about McCann and that little Irishman stealing his horses? How did all that take place?"

"I don't know," Davis said. "I've never heard Carlton talk about it. I'm beginning to wonder."

"Does it matter now?" Lenke asked. "This McCann fellow shot a federal marshal. We're after him and we should stay after him, all of us, together."

Davis turned to Lenke. "What do you know about McCann?"

Lenke was fidgeting. "I heard the people talking."

"What were they saying?" Davis asked.

Lenke fidgeted more. "They said he shot Hank Trent so fast that Trent didn't know what killed him. They said Trent had his pistol out, aimed at McCann, and McCann pulled and emptied his gun. Can you imagine that? Hank Trent didn't have a chance."

"You can hear a lot of things," Davis said. "How much of it is true is another thing."

"Well," Lenke said, "it's a fact that Trent was shot down. You can't argue that. I say that McCann fellow is very dangerous and that we should all stay together and get him."

"The problem is, Ruz doesn't want us to stay together," Davis pointed out. "He's never wanted us with him. So there's no reason to think he's even on our side."

"He's on his own side," Jones put in. "I don't think he even cares anything for Carlton. For some reason, he's really got it in for us."

"He's an Indian and he hates us," Davis said. "That's all there is to it."

"He hates you most, Mr. Davis," Lenke said. "Maybe you say too much to him."

"Maybe you say too much," Davis told Lenke. "What is it? Are you part Indian or something?"

"That doesn't matter to me," Lenke said. "I have said that I think we should be after this McCann fellow. Not each other."

Everyone agreed that Lenke had a point. McCann would love it if he knew what was happening within the posse. Jones thought the real reason for Ruz's anger was that Davis was a leader, and Ruz didn't want anyone leading but him.

"I'm no gunman," Davis said, "but I'm about to make a play on Ruz. I've come to believe it's either him or me."

Jones agreed. "I'd say you're right, Will. And I go as far as to say that the rest of us are in trouble as well. If we're all smart, we'll back you."

"I don't think we should make trouble now," Lenke repeated. "We've come so far, and Ruz said that for sure we should find them tomorrow. Maybe we should try and keep peace."

"Why did you even come along?" Jones asked Lenke. "Can you even shoot a gun?"

Lenke stiffened. "I've fought for my family before, yes. I'm here because I don't want men like that McCann running the streets of our town, making trouble."

"I'm beginning to wonder who is making the most trouble," Davis said. "Somehow I don't think anyone could be worse than Ruz."

"Maybe this McCann fellow," Lenke said.

"Do you know McCann at all?" Davis asked.

"No," Lenke replied.

"But you've been around Ruz for a while now, haven't you?"

"Well, yes, of course."

"Tell me, then, Mr. Lenke, have you ever met a man who would rather bet his fingers than money?"

"No, I have never met a man like that."

"So wouldn't you say that Ruz was every bit as dangerous to us as McCann?"

Lenke felt trapped. His raised his voice. "I'm telling you, if you'll just leave him alone and let him lead us, he won't hurt anyone. He just doesn't like you pushing him."

Jones turned to Davis. He pointed at Lenke and laughed. "He must be part Indian. He won't even listen."

Lenke sat back and took a deep breath. He got up and started away.

"Don't leave yet," Davis told him.

Lenke turned. "Why not?"

"Because this meeting's not finished yet."

"I don't think I have to be in on it any longer," Lenke said.

Davis stood up. "I'll need to ask you a question, then." He studied the shopkeeper. "If trouble comes, will you side with us or Ruz and Carlton?"

"If trouble comes, I will stay out of it," Lenke said.

"Are you taking Ruz's side?"

"I'm taking no one's side. I believe that we all came out here together and that we should all stay together and quit these problems."

"Do you intend to say anything to Ruz or Carlton about this talk we're having?" Jones asked.

Lenke fidgeted. "No. Nothing."

"That's good," Davis said. "Because if Ruz or Carlton either one learn what we've said, we'll all know it was you who told them."

"Don't be insane!" Lenke's face was drawn tight. "I don't want trouble. I wouldn't be a fool and cause it."

"I just wanted to be sure," Davis said. "This problem with Ruz is at the boiling point. Anything could happen."

"Well, I don't know why it's this way," Lenke said, "but I wouldn't be foolish enough to make things worse." He turned and walked to the edge of camp and sat down.

Davis sat down with the others by the fire. "I don't know about him."

"He's harmless," Jones said. "But I've been wondering why things are this way, and what Ruz and Carlton are off talking about. Do you suppose they'd get rid of us after we helped get McCann and the others?"

"Seven fifty a day, per man, isn't that much," Davis said. "Besides, it's not out of their pockets."

"Well, what if there's a reward for McCann and the other two?" Jones suggested. "Maybe Carlton would like to collect that and split it with Ruz. With us around, they'd have to split it again."

Davis thought a moment. "I wonder, too. You know, I'm going to go and find Mr. Ruz and Mr. Carlton. And when I find them, I'm going to ask them some questions that I want answers to."

Eleven

Carlton realized that sitting in the darkness, building hate for Joel McCann, would neither bring his brother back nor get McCann. It was getting late and Carlton knew he needed rest to be able to get through the next day. Then he would get McCann and hope that he felt better somehow.

He jumped suddenly as Ruz knelt down beside him and said, "Let's leave. Now."

Carlton regained his composure. "Why did you sneak up like that?"

"I don't want the others hearing us," Ruz said. "They're gathered around the fire, talking. I think we should ride out. Right now."

"What are you talking about?"

"You and me," Ruz said. "Let's go. Now."

"You mean leave the posse here?"

"Yes."

"And travel in the dark? You can't track them now."

"I don't need to. I know where they're at. I know where they're going." Ruz was sitting down, talking low. "The trail they've taken goes up Timpas Creek and over the top. There's no other way unless they backtrack and go down again. We can catch them in their bedrolls if we leave now."

"You're sure of that?"

"Yes," Ruz said. "I'm sure of where they are and I think we're better off in the dark. I've been thinking on it. I don't want McCann shooting at me in the daylight with that Sharps."

"That's a good point," Carlton said. "But what about the others? We promised to pay them."

"*You* promised to pay them," Ruz hissed. "There's not a one of them I would pay even a handful of flour."

"What if they come after us and want their money?" Carlton asked.

"Don't be so worried," Ruz said. He heard a sound and stood up quickly, pulling his knife.

Carlton came to his feet and saw Davis standing in the shadows.

"Fine way to greet someone," Davis said to Ruz.

"What are you doing here?" Ruz asked.

"I was going to ask you two the same question. I woke up and saw that you were both gone. I checked the horses and nobody's watching them. I thought you were supposed to be watching them, Ruz."

"You don't worry about me," Ruz said.

"I'm worried about the horses," Davis said. "What if McCann decided to double back and steal them? He'd have them by now."

"Listen," Ruz said, "I told you not to worry about it."

"Easy," Carlton said. "There's no need for any problems."

"We've already got problems," Davis said. "A lot of them. You two out here talking has got us to wondering. We've been thinking that maybe there's already a reward out on McCann and that you two plan to divvy it up, leaving us out."

"I don't know about any reward," Carlton said. "Even if there was, the rest of you wouldn't be entitled to any of it."

"Why not?"

"Because our deal was seven fifty a day, that's why. We didn't discuss any reward money. Besides, I doubt there is any. It's too early. If we were to go back without catching McCann, that would be different. But we're going to catch him, if you and the others would quit causing problems."

Ruz was staring at Davis. Carlton asked him to put the knife away. Ruz felt the blade and sheathed it, mumbling in Apache and Spanish.

"I still don't like you two leaving camp," Davis insisted. "It makes me think there's secrets between you."

"We've been talking about leaving right away," Carlton said. "That's why we're out here. We didn't want to wake you until we talked about it. And we've decided that we'll go just as soon as the horses are saddled."

"We're breaking camp?" Davis asked. "What for? It's not even close to daylight."

"We'll lose them otherwise," Carlton said. "Ruz knows where they are. We're going to hit them at dawn, before they get going. We can end this."

Davis went back to tell the others. Ruz pulled his knife again and threw it. The blade stuck in a nearby pine.

"What's the matter with you?" Carlton asked.

"I was hoping to get out of here without them. Now we're going to have the same problems we've been having all along, and it'll cause us to lose him if we're not careful."

"Then why didn't you just leave by yourself without telling me?" Carlton asked. "You could've snuck to the horses and been gone before I could've stopped you." When Ruz didn't answer, Carlton added, "Is it because you're not sure of McCann? Do you think, maybe, that you couldn't take him and the other two by yourself?"

"Why should I worry about the other two?" Ruz pulled his knife from the pine trunk.

"I should say, then, you're worried about McCann, that he's too good to handle alone. Isn't that what's bothering you here?"

"Maybe I'm worried about McCann," Ruz admitted. "I thought maybe there should be the two of us. Maybe I'm worried, just a little bit."

"Now you can see why I've thought we needed the others all along," Carlton said. "If you hadn't made enemies of them, we could be working together well right now. We could get McCann without any problems."

"I didn't say the others would be that much help," Ruz argued. "Cowpunchers and a shopkeeper. What kind of fighters are they?"

"Maybe they don't have to fight that much to be of help," Carlton said. "It's the numbers that count. I've been saying that all along."

"Maybe if we split them up, they could draw

McCann's fire," Ruz suggested. "Then we could get him."

"Now you're starting to think a little bit," Carlton said. "I don't care how we use the posse, but we need them."

"Then we'll use them the way I think we need to," Ruz said. "But we'd better get going or it will be too late even for that."

The moon was half-full, nearing midsky, giving off good light. Even so, the trail was treacherous and the going was much slower than Ruz could tolerate. He had to stop often to wait for posse members, which infuriated him.

The forest was cool and still, with not even a breeze. Every snort from a horse, every creak of saddle leather, drove Ruz closer to madness. He mumbled constantly.

During a climb through a rocky area, a horse caught its leg and fell, rolling and twisting over its rider. The rider, Cal Ritter, grabbed his lower leg and began yelling.

Ruz jumped down from his horse and drew his knife. He put the blade against Ritter's throat.

"You stop that noise! Do you understand me?"

Cal Ritter held his breath. In the moonlight, sweat beaded on his brow.

"There's no call for that," Davis said.

Ruz turned. "I don't want him yelling."

"We can't be that close to them yet."

"I don't care how close we are. He's too loud."

"You're going too far here," Davis said. "I've about had enough."

"We haven't got time for an argument," Carlton broke in. He knelt beside Cal Ritter. "Can you ride?"

"No," Ritter said. "My leg's broke. I can feel the bone. It's pushed through the skin."

The horse, its saddle twisted awkwardly on its back, was lying on its side, breathing heavily. One of its legs was also broken.

Clint Ritter was at his brother's side, visibly distressed. "What do we do now?" he asked Carlton.

"If he can't ride, he can't go any farther," Carlton said.

"You can't leave him here," Clint Ritter said.

"He'll be fine until we come back through," Carlton said. "Likely we'll be back by late morning. He'll get his full pay."

"I'll stay with him," Clint Ritter said.

"You won't get paid," Carlton said. "We need you up on the pass with us."

Cal Ritter, weeping and holding his leg, said, "Clint, you go on with them. I'll be fine until you get back."

"I don't care about the money," Clint Ritter said. "This is no way to leave you. I won't do it."

"What do you figure you can do for him?" Carlton asked.

"I've splinted broken bones before," Clint Ritter replied. "I'll take care of him until you get back. Maybe I'll get him down a ways."

"Do what you have to," Carlton said. He looked at the fallen horse. Clint Ritter stood up and pulled his pistol.

"No," Carlton said. "Don't shoot the horse until daybreak. By that time we'll have gotten McCann and the others."

"I'll just put it in his ear. There won't be much noise."

Carlton was insistent. "We don't want them hearing us. Just do as I say and wait until daybreak. Wait until the sun's up. We'll have gotten McCann for sure by then."

Clint Ritter holstered his pistol and went back to his brother. "He's not doing so well. How long did you say you'd be up there?"

"I want to get it done at daybreak," Carlton said. "We'll be back as soon as we can."

"We can't wait here too long," Clint Ritter said. "Cal's feeling poorly and he won't get better till we find a doc."

"We'll get him to one, don't worry," Carlton promised. "Just stay with him."

"Let's go!" Ruz said. "We've lost a lot of time already."

Carlton mounted and they fell into line behind Ruz, leaving Clint Ritter tending to his moaning brother. Carlton didn't give much chance to a man whose leg was broken that badly, being so far from a doctor. But it didn't really matter. The only thing that was important now was getting McCann.

Again, Ruz was in the lead, but riding at a controlled pace. They had lost precious time. Carlton was aware of Ruz's rage. But Ruz had brought it on himself. Ruz had been leading them at too fast a pace through the rocky area.

He should have known better. None of these men were used to riding through country like this. Now Ruz would have no choice but to go slower, so that another accident didn't hold them up further.

Carlton realized that Ruz was now riddled with interior conflict. Ruz had said that he didn't think that he could get McCann and the other two by himself and thought he needed help. Still, he couldn't stand the string of problems that delayed them so often. He wanted to do it alone, yet for the first time he wasn't sure that he could.

Carlton wondered if he himself hadn't made a mistake. He thought about his decision to come to Cimarron in the first place. It had seemed like a good choice, an easy way of getting rid of McCann and Devlin. It hadn't worked out so easily, though, and now things had become increasingly complicated.

In the east, a hint of gray appeared. Carlton wondered how close they were to reaching McCann. He couldn't tell a thing by Ruz, who continued ahead and never looked back.

Carlton turned to see Davis and Jones talking in low whispers. The shopkeeper, Lenke, rode up next to Carlton and asked if his widow would get his payment if he was killed.

"What are you talking about?" Carlton asked. Lenke's voice unnerved him. It was as if Lenke knew something was going to happen.

"I want my wife to have my payment," he repeated. "If I die, I want her to have it."

"Sure," Carlton said, "I'll see to it. But why are you worried? We've got five, and there are but three of them."

"There were seven of us," Lenke pointed out. "That Ritter boy will surely die. I didn't like it when he fell. I didn't like the yelling."

"Nobody liked it," Carlton said. "Accidents happen."

"Mr. Ruz wasn't thinking. He shouldn't have taken us through those rocks in the dark."

"He's been through there a hundred times," Carlton said. "He didn't see a problem. And if that boy hadn't been so scared, there wouldn't have been a problem."

Lenke shook his head. "It's not a good sign."

"I wouldn't worry about it."

"I shouldn't worry? Why shouldn't I worry when you are? You and Mr. Ruz are both worried."

"What are you talking about?"

"I've been watching you both," Lenke said. "You have problems with each other. No one knows quite what to do about this McCann, this dangerous man. Don't you think that I can tell you're both worried?"

"It's just a hard chase, is all," Carlton said. "Nobody's worried."

Lenke rode silent a moment. "I just want you to promise me that you'll give my pay to my wife."

"Whatever you want," Carlton said. "We'd better ride quiet now. We should be getting pretty close to their camp."

"Sure," Lenke said. "I'm glad you know where we are. It makes me feel so much better."

Carlton studied him in the darkness. "You're not going crazy on me, are you?"

"No, no," Lenke said. "I'd never go crazy. Everybody in the posse is fighting everybody else, except that dangerous man that we came to find, that Mr. McCann. He's the one that we should be fighting, not one another. Isn't there enough fighting each other to make anyone crazy?"

"Yeah, maybe there is," Carlton agreed. "But it's a little late to worry about it now. Just take it easy."

Lenke dropped back and Carlton looked ahead for a sign from Ruz. No sign. Ruz just continued to ride, never looking back.

In the east, the gray widened. In very little time it would be light. Carlton began to panic. Where were they? Were they close to McCann's camp? Why didn't Ruz stop and say something to him?

Lenke wasn't that far off. Everything that was going on was insane: Ruz and his rage, the mumbling, and pulling his knife all the time. And Davis with his mistrust and demanding attitude. Maybe Lenke was the only sane one in the bunch.

Thinking of his brother again, Carlton wished he had stayed in the street when McCann and the other two had made their escape from the jail. He could at least have taken a few shots and maybe have gotten lucky. Then he wouldn't be here, in this mess, wondering what was going to happen next.

He realized that now he would never know if he could have killed McCann. He had turned and had ridden up a side street, thinking at the time that McCann would surely have killed him. The way he felt now, a quick death would have been better than this slow one riding through this country.

The gray light widened. Ruz didn't turn around, didn't say a word. Carlton believed that as it stood now, there was little chance of getting McCann in his sleep. There probably had never been much chance of that. McCann traveled like Ruz, like an Indian. Maybe that's what was upsetting Ruz so much.

Carlton began to worry now that McCann might be waiting for them, resting the Sharps over a rock or a tree snag. That gun could shoot a long way.

Carlton decided that he couldn't change anything now. They would use the rest of the posse as decoys and hope that McCann showed himself. It was a slim chance, to say the least, but the only one they had.

Twelve

As the sun rose, McCann made his way through the timber to an overlook. He had been up since daybreak, listening, watching. Nothing had told him there was a posse near. Not yet, anyway.

The day was beginning open and peaceful. The birds were singing and the air was still cool. It wouldn't be long, though, until things changed.

At the overlook, McCann studied the country ahead of them. Some three miles up the trail, through the dawn shadows, a large butte stood by itself. McCann wondered if it might be a sacred site to the Indians who once lived here, a place to go to fast and talk with the spirits.

McCann knew that a good distance beyond was Raton Pass, a notch in the rocky hills of oak and piñon pine, the door to Colorado. He had never ridden this way before, but he knew it would take them at least half a day to get there. Even across the border, McCann knew they wouldn't be safe from the posse.

Carlton would go to any lengths to have someone else do his work for him, McCann thought. Otherwise he wouldn't have gone to Cimarron to do a job he might have done himself along the trail.

He could have set himself up in ambush, if he had known how to do it. Likely he didn't know how, or was too afraid of missing. Carlton wasn't one to face a man straight on.

McCann turned from the butte to look over the mountains behind them, the spreading light bathing the land in soft gold. The oaks and piñons were thick and green, clinging to rocky slopes and mountainsides. Way out, the arroyos along the bottom looked like crooked lines carved through a vast, brush-covered gray blanket.

As McCann watched, he noted jays scolding and flitting among the pines a distance down the slope. Something was disturbing them.

A thin film of dust rose from the trees where the jays were gathered. The posse had drawn very close. He could see them now, less than two miles back, Ruz in the lead, riding single file up the trail.

McCann lowered himself from his position. Back in camp, he spoke softly. "The posse's nearly caught us. I'm going to double back and slow them up. Corky, you make for Raton Pass and don't look back. Martha, stay with him. Ride as hard as you have to. I'll catch you both when I'm done."

"You can't do it alone," Martha said. "There's too many of them."

"I intend to drop a couple of them," McCann said. "It might scare some of the others away. Besides, Carlton and Ruz are the only two that I'm worried about."

"You're not taking the others for granted, are you?" Martha warned. "You don't know anything about them."

"And they'll be waiting for you, lad," Corky said. "They'll figure you to come back. Ruz would know that."

"It doesn't matter one way or the other," McCann said. "They're getting too close. We can't have that."

"They'll surround you," Martha protested. "I don't think you should go alone. I think we should all make a stand and fight them together."

"I agree with her, I surely do," Devlin said. He was squeezing his empty bottle. "It's not often that I agree with a woman. But I do this time."

"It looks like I'm outnumbered," McCann said. "Maybe if we work this right, we can put the run on them."

"Where can we make a stand?" Corky asked.

McCann pointed ahead. "There's a big butte about three miles up. That will be as good a place as any."

McCann checked the big Sharps rifle, and the smaller Henry repeater. He made sure Martha's rifle was in good working order. Devlin was checking his own rifle, cradling the whiskey bottle under one arm.

"Why are you keeping that bottle?" McCann asked him. "There's nothing in it."

"I told you, lad, I like to pretend there is," Corky said. "It makes me feel better. And I really need it now, you know."

They mounted and began riding as hard as they could. The horses could rest once they reached the butte.

As they neared the butte, McCann began to study

the country. The trail to the butte crossed an open meadow. The posse would have to expose themselves for a good distance before they reached the butte, and would then have to climb a steep trail to reach the top.

"It will be a good place to make our stand," McCann said. "But we have to shoot well and then leave. We can't stay up there. We'll be trapped. If they surround us, they'll hold us there until we're starved out."

The sun had risen fully and the ride up the butte's side was hot. It made them want to get back into the trees. The only good thing about it, the heat kept the rattlesnakes tight in the brush or in their dens underground.

At the top, they met the trees again, the wonderful trees, where a breeze felt cool and a trickle of water flowed from a little spring. It would have been a good place to stay if the posse weren't closing in.

McCann checked the Sharps again. He picked an overlook and studied the country, noting where the trail left cover to cross the open. No matter how they rode, they had to cross the open to get around the butte.

"I can see it now, lad," Corky said. "They'll be sitting ducks out there."

"They won't sit that still," McCann said.

Martha squinted. "Can you shoot that far?"

"Yes, I can shoot that far," McCann said. "This rifle will reach a long way."

Martha studied the rifle. She had heard of a Sharps, and had seen a few, but had never seen one fired.

"They're for hunting buffalo, aren't they?" she asked.

"That's what they're made for," McCann said. "They'll shoot over a mile. But it's not nearly that far to the trees down there. Probably less than a half mile."

"Do they know you can shoot them from here?"

"I imagine. With any luck, they won't know we're up here." He laughed at himself. "But that's wishful thinking. There's no doubt they'll be cautious. Ruz might even be thinking about it in the back of his mind."

Devlin was holding his empty whiskey bottle. He rubbed it between his hands. "How far back are they, do you figure?"

"They'll be here any minute," McCann replied.

Devlin studied the trail from the butte back down to the pines. "Do you really think they'll cross the open down there?"

"There's no other way to Raton Pass, not unless they double back and take another trail a long way down. They won't want to lose the time."

Corky shook his head. He uncorked his bottle of water and drank deeply. "It's the wrong color, for certain," he said, "but it tastes mighty good."

"We'll fill all the water bags and be ready to move fast," McCann said. "Once they know I'm up here with the Sharps, it should slow them down. Then we can go down the back side and gain some time on them."

"You get the first one," Corky said, "and the rest might go home."

"I hope so," McCann said. "I hope Ruz rides out first. That would help us a lot. If Ruz was gone, that would make a lot of difference. Carlton won't know what to do. We might even be able to relax."

Ruz stood swatting the reins against his pants leg, cursing, while his horse drank deeply of the cool mountain water. "We missed them. Damned if we didn't just miss them."

They were at the headwaters of Timpas Creek. The ashes from McCann's fire were still warm.

This has been what Ruz had wanted to avoid. He knew that if they missed getting McCann before light, the chase would then be very hard. McCann would find a large butte not far ahead, a butte the Indians called Thunder's Home. If McCann got up there, he could shoot the Sharps a long way.

Ruz had decided a long way back that he wouldn't tell anyone about the butte. This, he would keep to himself.

Ruz continued to curse, yelling for the others to hurry and get their horses watered. He didn't care how loud he was now. McCann would know they were very near.

Near Ruz stood Carlton, contemplating their next move while his horse cropped grass. Besides not catching up with McCann, there was another problem: Davis was still making trouble. He and Jones were over near a large pine and they were discussing something in low, angry voices.

A short distance away, Lenke stood looking out over the timber, his hat in his hand. Carlton wondered if he wasn't praying, or saying some kind of good-bye.

Ruz yelled again for the posse to mount up. Lenke climbed into the saddle. Davis and Jones ignored him.

"Now, see this problem we've got," Ruz said to Carlton. "Am I going to have to shoot that cowpuncher's fingers off, like I promised?"

"You'll have to take it up with him," Carlton said. "But I'll back you."

At the large pine, Davis and Jones continued to

talk. Ruz led the way over, with Carlton behind, and stood firmly in front of Davis.

"We haven't got time to waste," Ruz told Davis. "Get on your horse."

"What's the use?" Davis said. "We've been riding night and day, and we still haven't caught them. We were thinking that it might be too late, since we're so close to Colorado."

"You knew it would be hard when you signed on," Carlton said. "You shouldn't be complaining."

"We should've caught them by now," Davis said. "Ruz led us to believe we'd get them by daybreak. It should be over. Maybe we'll never get them."

"We'll catch them," Carlton said. "We're close now. They're just ahead."

"Do you know that for sure?" Davis asked.

Ruz said, "We know that for sure. Take my word for it. You can come along or go. Either way, it doesn't matter."

"You've come a long way," Carlton said. "Why would you want to quit now?"

Jones told Carlton, "Once they get over Raton Pass, we can't catch them. They'll reach Colorado."

"I told you when we left," Carlton said, "we'll go into Colorado after them. Since they killed Trent, it's a federal matter."

"We've been talking about that," Davis said. "When did you get a warrant for their arrest? You can't cross state lines without a warrant."

"We'll get the warrant after we catch them," Carlton said. "It's important that we get them. We'll worry about the paperwork later. Why don't you remember? You knew that when we left."

"You didn't say that when we left," Davis argued. "You're saying it for the first time now."

Carlton frowned. He pointed to Ruz. "He said it. He's the deputy. You calling him a liar?"

Davis stared at Carlton. "I'm calling *you* a liar. Leave Ruz out of it."

"If you call him a liar, you call me a liar," Ruz said.

Jones shook his head. "It's not worth all this. Let's just turn back."

"Maybe you're right," Davis said. "I don't like how this is going, and it's not worth a fight. We'll just draw our pay and ride out."

"If you go, you're not getting paid," Carlton said.

"We put in a day apiece," Davis insisted. "That's seven fifty each."

"No," Carlton said. "You get paid only if you stay on to help catch them. You leave now and there's no money in it for either of you."

A short distance away, Lenke sat his horse, staring out over the mountains.

Davis glared at Carlton. "You didn't make that plain in the beginning. You said seven fifty a day. You said we'd get paid on the spot, when the job was done. That's what you said."

Ruz spoke up. "Maybe you didn't hear right back in Cimarron."

"I heard right," Davis said.

"I'm making it plain now. No pay," Ruz said, his hand on his pistol.

Jones suddenly went for his gun. But Ruz had already pulled his and shot Jones in the stomach. Jones went down, belching, and lay doubled up. Ruz shot him twice more.

Lenke screamed. He kicked his horse into a dead run through the trees. Carlton pulled his pistol and emptied it at Lenke.

Lenke doubled over the saddle but didn't fall. His horse continued to run. Ruz kept his pistol trained on Davis.

Davis just stared. He knelt down next to his cousin, who arched his back and died.

Davis rose slowly, glaring at Ruz and Carlton.

"You're both killers. Why did you even bother to take anyone else along?"

Ruz aimed the pistol at Davis. "Hold up your right hand."

"What?"

"I told you if you gave me any more trouble, I'd shoot your fingers off. Now, hold out your hand. Either that, or I'll just kill you."

Carlton stepped in. "Wait. You don't want to kill him."

Ruz pushed him back. "Stay out of this."

"Ruz, it would be stupid to kill him, or even shoot his fingers off."

"Why?" Ruz asked.

"We talked about it earlier. McCann has a Sharps and he'll be waiting for us. Do you want to be leading the way?"

Ruz remembered their discussion about using the rest of the posse as decoys. Maybe he shouldn't have shot Jones. Maybe Lenke wouldn't have ridden off like a madman.

But Carlton was right. Davis would be useful. In his mind Ruz could see the butte rising from the forest floor just ahead. He had been thinking about that. McCann wouldn't pass up a chance to try and slow them down. The man in the lead would be a prime target. For once, maybe Carlton had a good idea.

Thirteen

McCann watched the trail that came out from the timber toward the butte. He was intent and uneasy. By his calculations, Carlton and Ruz should have already arrived.

Something had to be holding them up.

Then, in the distance, he heard popping sounds. Gunshots, muffled by the timber and the distance, yet distinct in the windless morning silence.

Devlin was dozing. McCann rousted him. "Wake up, Corky. Something's going to happen here any minute."

"Can't leave a man to sleep, can you, lad?" Devlin grumbled. "Hate to see a man get rest, don't you?"

"I heard gunshots, Corky. I can't figure why."

"You take care of them, lad," Devlin said, trying to lie down again. "I trust you greatly."

McCann insisted he stay awake, telling him, "You can sleep another time, when we're out of this mess."

Devlin sat up. "Where's Martha?"

"She's been gone awhile," McCann said.

"She's a smart one, she is," Devlin commented. "She knows enough to go off a piece to get some rest, without having the likes of you around."

"Do you want Carlton and Ruz catching up with us, and everyone be sleeping?" McCann asked. Devlin's lack of sleep had not only made him irritable, but reckless as well.

"Maybe they're sleeping in a bit, as well," Devlin said. He studied McCann. "Not likely, though. Aye, lad?"

"Not likely," McCann said.

Martha still hadn't returned. McCann began to wonder about her, and with Devlin awake, he decided to go and look for her.

"You watch the trail while I go find her," McCann said. "I'll be right back."

"What if they come while you're gone?" Devlin asked. "I'd hate to shoot the lot of them and you miss out."

"I'll be within eyesight," McCann said. "If they come, raise your rifle in the air."

Devlin was still mumbling as he took McCann's place at the observation point. McCann walked past the horses toward a thicket of trees and brush.

"I'm in here," Martha said. "What with the fresh water, I decided to take a bath."

"Take a bath?" McCann said. "You haven't got time for that."

"I just wanted a quick one," Martha said. "I felt pretty grimy. I'm finished now."

"I just heard gunshots," McCann said. "We've got to hurry back. I left Corky watching the trail and he's liable to fall asleep."

Martha hurried from the bushes. She had climbed into her skirt and was buttoning up her blouse. "I'm sorry. I know I shouldn't have, but the water looked so inviting."

Her skin was damp from the bath and she smelled of wild roses. He noticed some petals still clinging to her neck.

"I didn't have any perfume," she said when he asked her. "There were some roses blooming beside the spring. They seem to work, wouldn't you say?"

"Yes, they work real well," McCann said. "We'd better get back to Corky."

McCann hurried ahead, with Martha behind. At the observation point, Corky was snoring loudly.

McCann shook him awake. "I thought you were watching."

"Nobody's come, lad."

"How would you know?"

McCann looked down to where the trail came out of the trees. The trail was clear. He looked all along the side of the butte, where the trail led. Still, he could see none of the posse.

"I can't understand where that posse is," McCann said.

"Maybe you dreamed about them, lad," Devlin suggested. "Maybe you didn't see them a-tall."

"I saw them."

Devlin winked at Martha. "Oh, you've been known to be wrong, you have. You might not admit it, lad, but it's true."

"I saw them," McCann insisted. "There's no doubt in my mind."

"Well, they must have stopped for a Sunday outing," Devlin said.

"Is that them?" Martha asked, pointing.

McCann and Devlin both leaned forward. A rider had appeared from the trees, his horse at a walk, coming up the trail toward the butte.

The rider was leaning over the saddle and still too far away for them to tell if it was either Carlton or Ruz. The rider appeared to be alone, and there were no signs of the other posse members.

"What do you make of that?" Devlin asked.

"I wonder if he isn't a decoy," McCann said. "He's riding funny, though, like he's been injured."

Devlin laughed. "He can't do us a whole lot of harm that way, now can he?"

"Maybe it's a trick," Martha suggested.

"Whoever's on the horse is a card shy of a full deck," Devlin said. "He'll go down for sure."

"Maybe he figures I'll miss," McCann said. "If he draws our fire, that will tell Carlton and Ruz right where we are."

"Why would he volunteer to do that?" Martha asked. "That's suicide."

"You've got a point there," McCann said. "Let me think on this a bit."

"I know what to do," Martha said. "I think Corky and I should start down off the butte. We'll see what he does."

"What?" Corky said. "You can't be serious."

"I think it's a good idea," Martha continued. "Maybe Carlton and Ruz are hiding somewhere, watching to see what happens to that lone rider. If we start down, maybe the rest of them will come out."

"Yes," Corky said. "Maybe they'll come out and shoot us. I'd rather be shooting at them."

Martha looked to McCann. "Can you shoot anyone who comes toward us before they're in range to shoot at us?"

"Yes, I believe I can. I don't like taking that chance, though."

"What chance is there?" Martha said. "We start down. If that rider starts something, Corky and I can shoot him. If Carlton and Ruz come out after us, you do your business with the big rifle. If we get in danger, we'll just turn around and ride back up."

"Carlton and Ruz know I have the rifle," McCann said. He was watching the rider, coming ever closer. "I don't think they'll put themselves out in the open if they can help it. They might wait long enough for you two to get down on the bottom."

Martha pointed to the other end of the butte. "If they don't come out right away when Corky and I leave, then why don't you follow us down? Then, if they show, you can open fire on them. We can ride to the other end of the butte if we have to, can't we?"

"We could make a stand at the other end, yes," McCann said. "The way it's looking now, that might be better. But having you and Corky in plain sight is living pretty dangerously."

"It's been dangerous since we left," Martha said. "It can't be any more dangerous now."

Ruz rode in front and Carlton followed, leading Davis's horse. They rode at a gallop, hurrying to catch up with Lenke.

Davis was tied to the saddle. He knew what the plans were. Ruz and Carlton had been talking about how they would use him as a decoy by sending him out into the open, toward the butte that lay just ahead.

At first Davis had cared very little about what happened. He had believed he was going to die anyway, and had been numbed with shock from losing his cousin, who hadn't even gotten a decent burial.

Even if he lived, he reasoned, he couldn't go to Texas anyway. He had told the trail boss he would bring four of them to work a herd of longhorns toward Kansas. Even if Cal Ritter survived his broken leg, he wouldn't be able to ride for a long time. And Clint wouldn't go without his brother.

Then Davis's apathy had turned to raging anger. Ruz had whipped him with a rope when he hadn't put his hands out to be tied, and had again threatened to shoot his fingers off. Davis had resigned himself to going along with what he was told, but had vowed that Ruz and Carlton would die with him.

As they rode, Davis tried to understand how everything had gotten so complicated. Seven fifty a day for a month wasn't worth the loss of his cousin. The Ritters were good boys, but neither of them had ever herded cattle before, and certainly neither of them had ever been on a manhunt.

Davis thought about the two men ahead of him. Carlton was as big a coward as ever squirmed out from under a rock. He liked to see men die; but he didn't want to take any chances doing it himself.

Ruz, always muttering in Spanish and Apache, cared more for blood than anything else. You couldn't tell how crazy this man was until you got out on the trail with him. In town he had been quiet and had let Carlton do all the talking. You could tell from the beginning, though, that he hadn't liked the idea of a posse.

It was too late to relive all that now, Davis thought. Hindsight was a lost cause. The best thing to do was to plan how to get Carlton and Ruz killed along with himself. They deserved it more than he did, and certainly more than Jones and the Ritter boys.

And what about Lenke? He had ridden away with bullets in his back. So far there hadn't been any gunshots up ahead, and they hadn't run into him lying on the ground, or his horse grazing by itself anywhere.

Ruz and Carlton slowed their horses. The butte lay just ahead, where they both believed McCann might be waiting for them.

"If we had the whole posse left, we could take the butte from two sides," Carlton said, tying the reins on Davis's saddle. "But you had to whittle everybody down so that we've got one man left."

"I told you that there'd be trouble," Ruz answered him. "And I told you that if we had trouble, I'd blame you."

Davis smiled to himself. He had known all along that those two had had their differences. He just hadn't known how far apart they really were. By the sounds of it, they had come to hate one another almost as bad as he hated them.

And they didn't seem to be worried that he could hear them. Maybe they thought he was harmless, with his hands tied behind him. Maybe they thought he was about to do them some good and die in the process, so it didn't matter what they said in front of him.

He smiled to himself. They were so very wrong.

Carlton finished tying the reins to Davis's saddle. As Carlton and Ruz continued to talk, Davis studied the country ahead. They were approaching a clearing, and he could hear Ruz telling Carlton that the butte was less than a half mile away. It was time to act.

Davis kicked his horse hard. The horse jumped forward into a dead run, with Davis leaning forward over the saddle. He could hear Carlton and Ruz yelling and he could hear shooting behind him, and shooting ahead of him. Bullets whistled over his head from both directions. He was in a cross fire, and he knew there was no way out.

Fourteen

McCann had been watching the trail where it left the trees. Something was very odd. Since the first rider, none of the other posse members had appeared. The first rider had fallen from his horse and was lying still in the trail.

Martha and Devlin had left for the bottom of the butte, riding slowly, watching carefully. Still, no one had appeared.

McCann's mind worked, summing up that the posse had been fighting among themselves and a gunfight had taken place. McCann had seen it before. Nothing that unusual among greedy men.

Just below, Martha and Devlin were nearing the bottom of the butte when three riders appeared at the edge of the clearing. Suddenly one of the three riders burst from the timber, leaning low over his horse.

As the rider left the trees, McCann could see that one of the remaining two men was shooting at him. It was Ruz. He was riding a small, stout black pinto. McCann was now certain that infighting had occurred.

McCann waved and yelled for Martha and Devlin to come back up. Instead, they dismounted and aimed their rifles at the oncoming rider. McCann laid the Sharps across a rock and adjusted the sight for distance to the edge of the trees.

McCann could see that the oncoming rider was not Carlton. He had to be back at the trees with Ruz.

McCann aimed the Sharps and touched off. Ruz was turning his horse to return to cover when the big gun boomed. The large slug whizzed toward its target, hitting with a heavy whack.

McCann could see the horse lurch, rear, and go down, flailing out its last moments of life under a large pine.

McCann could see that Ruz was trapped under his dead pony. He watched as Carlton rode back farther into cover.

Ruz could free himself at any moment. McCann reloaded and fired. Another boom and, after a few moments, the slug tore into the pine just above Ruz's head.

Can't hurry this! McCann told himself. *Take your time and aim.*

McCann cocked the hammer back and took a deep breath. He squeezed off carefully. He blew the smoke aside and squinted, seeing Ruz jerk violently, fall back, and lie still.

* * *

Colorado Gold

Carlton stared with disbelief. Chico Ruz lay on his side, his mouth open in a silent scream. His bulging eyes were glazed over in death.

They should have stayed back in the trees and not shown even the slightest target. But Ruz had been eager to shoot Davis. After all that had happened, he hadn't wanted the cowpuncher to get away.

With McCann shooting that Sharps, and the other two shooting from the base of the butte, how could Davis have possibly gotten away?

Instead, it had been Ruz who had made the mistake. He had gotten too crazy. He had ridden out just a little ways, just far enough to get clear shots at Davis. And he had paid the price.

The first slug from the Sharps had come as a shock to both of them. It had slammed into Ruz's pony, just above the left shoulder. The horse had reared and had fallen, trapping Ruz against the base of a pine.

Ruz had yelled, "What? Why did he shoot at me? Why didn't he shoot Davis?"

Carlton, staying back in the trees, had yelled, "Ruz, you had better get your leg out from under that horse."

Ruz had been working to free himself, cursing in Apache and Spanish, yelling in pain. He had pulled his knife and had begun hacking at the horse's leg, trying to pull clear.

Carlton had wondered if maybe Ruz knew how Cal Ritter had felt after falling under his horse back in the rocks.

"You'd better hurry, Ruz!" Carlton had yelled, staying back. "He's going to shoot again."

Ruz had yelled to him, "Come and help me!" But Carlton hadn't moved.

The second shot had blown a branch from the pine right above Ruz's head. Splinters had showered down everywhere.

"Get over here and help me!" Ruz had screamed to Carlton. Still, Carlton hadn't moved.

The third shot had taken Ruz as he was cursing again. The slug had slammed into him just under his left shoulder, blowing his lungs out through his right rib cage.

Carlton now backed his horse farther into the trees. Out on the trail, Davis had fallen sideways on his horse. Still tied, he was bouncing like a loose sack of potatoes. The little man in the red derby was stopping his horse.

Carlton could hear another slug from the Sharps whizz through the trees near him, cutting through overhead branches. Carlton froze with fear. McCann couldn't possibly see him!

Carlton turned his horse and rode in the other direction at a dead run. He would ride down and out of the mountains and find another way into Colorado, any wagon road or trail that didn't have Joel McCann on it.

As he rode out, Carlton worried more than ever. He would have to find a telegraph office and wire Marvin Hurlan the news, something he didn't look forward to. Then he would have to reach Central City before McCann and Devlin and face Hurlan's wrath.

Hurlan would want to know everything, particularly why the job wasn't finished. He wanted all the mining claims he could get before the new smelting technology caught on and everyone realized that underground mining was soon to be profitable.

Carlton knew Hurlan would surely locate some

more gunmen. He would tell Hurlan how dangerous McCann was and talk him into going all out. Hurlan was sure to be as angry as he had ever been. It wouldn't be pleasant, but it would be better than trying to kill McCann by himself.

The rider was near dead, tied to the saddle, fallen to one side off his horse. Devlin held the horse and McCann cut the man loose, saying, "He looks to be a cowhand. I wonder why he joined a posse chasing us."

Davis lay on the ground, disoriented. Bleary-eyed, he looked up at McCann.

"Get those other two. Get them." He was shot twice through the lungs and his words were garbled.

"What did you say?" McCann asked.

"Ruz . . . Carlton." He struggled for more words. He took a painful breath and died.

"You're a straight shot, you are, ma'am," Devlin told Martha. "You did him in good, you did. I didn't even have to fire once."

Martha was looking the other way, feeling sick to her stomach. She had never killed before. It had been instinctual, as Davis had come straight at her and Devlin.

She had taken a deep breath and had fired three times, hitting him twice. When she had seen that he was tied, she had become upset.

"You can't go blaming yourself, lass," Devlin had told her. "How was anybody to know? You did what you had to."

Martha hadn't been comforted. Earlier, she had talked so openly about riding down off the butte and taking the posse on. Now she wondered if she hadn't spoken too soon. Killing was something, she decided, that changed you forever.

As she wiped tears from her eyes, Martha said, "Why did any of this have to happen?"

McCann pulled Davis's eyelids down and rose to his feet. "A lot of things happen that folks don't ask for. Like Corky said, you can't blame yourself. You thought he was riding to shoot you. That's how it happened."

"So where is the rest of the posse?" Martha asked. "Are they waiting to ambush us?"

"I can't tell you," McCann said, looking around. "It's peculiar."

"They could be anywhere," Devlin said. "The fiends!"

"I know Ruz won't be bothering us any longer," McCann said. "But I don't know about Carlton, or the rest of them."

"You'd think they'd have fired on us by now," Devlin said. "Maybe they hightailed it out of here."

"You two ride back up on the butte," McCann told Martha and Devlin. "I'll ride over to the trees and see what I can find out."

"No, you're not going without us," Martha said.

"There's no use risking your life over there," McCann said.

"And there's no use in you risking yours."

"I have to see what's happened to the others."

"And you'll need help." Martha wasn't backing down. "Besides, what if you leave and they come after Corky and me?"

Corky winked. "She's got a point, lad."

"We should all stay together from here on," Martha said. "No more splitting up."

They mounted and McCann led the way along the

trail back to the trees. They passed Lenke's body and his horse, which grazed peacefully just off the trail.

McCann led them cautiously, stopping often to scout the area and listen for sounds of disturbance from the birds and squirrels. There was nothing to suggest anyone nearby.

When they reached the edge of the timber, McCann dismounted. Ruz and his horse lay still. Again, Martha looked away.

Corky stared and said, "That big gun does a lot of damage, I'd say. Good God in heaven, it does."

McCann studied the ground, noting that the most recent tracks had been made by just three horses.

"It looks to me like Carlton and Ruz had just the cowhand with them," he said. "I don't know what happened to the others. Maybe they turned back."

"Or maybe they got shot back there, where you heard the gunfire," Devlin suggested.

"Anything's possible," McCann said. "But we need to know where Carlton went."

McCann led his horse through the trees, following Carlton's tracks. Carlton had turned his horse around and had begun riding back the other way.

After a short distance, Carlton's tracks left the main trail for one that headed down out of the timber. McCann knew that Carlton had had enough and was headed north to Colorado, via a lower trail, to lick his wounds.

McCann rode back to Martha and Devlin. "It looks like we've got open riding, at least for a while. Carlton has decided to leave us alone for the time being."

"He's no doubt hightailing it back to Marvin

Hurlan," Devlin said. "Hurlan will be mighty unhappy with things."

"We'll have our hands full again in Central City," McCann said. "But before we get there, maybe I'll run into my wife and son somewhere along the way."

"And I can finally concentrate on catching up with my friends and my son," Martha added. "I hope they're not too worried. They were expecting me long before this."

"We'll get you down there to them," McCann promised. "After the help you've given us, I'll be certain you get back with your son."

McCann led the way once again, this time much more relaxed. They were no longer being chased, and all that separated them from Colorado was Raton Pass, a half-day's ride ahead.

They could camp peacefully that night, for a change, and look forward to a good night's sleep. Carlton had surely gone on to Central City.

But Carlton wouldn't be finished. He would soon find someone else to fight his battles and be looking for a place from where he could shoot somebody in the back. McCann just hoped he could get Martha to her boy and find Minnie and his son before the next round of gunfire started.

Fifteen

Marvin Hurlan stood at the window of his office, looking out at the rocky hills above Central City. His three-story Victorian mansion on Eureka Street was one of the finest homes in the gulch, complete with three maids and a butler.

Hurlan's spacious office encompassed one half of the first floor, the room where he spent most of his time. The remainder of the mansion was kept clean and tidy, but saw guests infrequently.

Known by everyone in Central City, Marvin Hurlan had a few friends and a lot of enemies. Among the miners especially, Hurlan was known as a hard man.

But Hurlan cared little about the miners. He had made a lot of powerful friends in the right places. He had been a partner in two major railroads built before the Rebellion and had learned how to use political ties to his benefit. He knew how merchandise was handled and how men got rich by buying and selling at the right time and place. He believed he could get men to work for him any time. Miners were a dime a dozen.

As Hurlan peered from his window, he puffed heavily on a large cigar, filling the room with smoke. The day was open and bright, and an early thunderstorm had left the mountains gleaming. But Hurlan was not enjoying the scenery.

Instead, he was trying to understand what was taking so long for Leon DuCain and the Carlton brothers to return from Carminga. They should have had ample time to take care of C.F. Devlin and Joel McCann.

Hurlan didn't want to think that anything had gone wrong. These two men, Devlin and McCann, had filed on a claim right next to his just before the war. They had called it the Molly Jordan.

There was a large gold vein that ran right below the surface on the Molly Jordan, extending deep into Gregory Hill, which contained massive lodes of ore. It could mean a lot of money to whoever owned the rights.

Hurlan had made lots of mining plans, and he wouldn't stand to have them changed. He had worked hard to get where he was, and at fifty-two, he stood to become one of the wealthiest men in Colorado. He liked that idea and would see to it that it came true.

Though the early gold rushes were now a thing of the past, and the gold on the surface had played out long ago, there was a new boom on its way to the gulch, which would greatly affect Central City. That

Colorado Gold

boom would come from a new technology to take the ore from the rock. A new gold rush was beginning, and Hurlan, as well as many others, was banking on the future of the new mining concept.

Whispers of the new concept had brought Hurlan to Denver in 1866. Then, a professor named Nathaniel Hill had come out from Brown University in the East and taken samples of ore to study in his laboratory. He had taken more samples across the ocean to Wales, where he had worked with scientists to perfect a method of smelting that would separate metals in rock.

Hurlan had kept track of Hill's work with interest. In 1867 Hill and his partners had built a smelter in Black Hawk, a sister mining town to Central City. A man named Peter McFarlane was planning a foundry in Central City. Other interests were springing up everywhere.

Hurlan was not about to be left out. He wanted his own foundry and enough ore to keep it producing enormous amounts of metal. Having the Molly Jordan mine would insure that he had plenty of profits.

Hurlan was already well in place. By setting up a partnership with some of his political friends in the East, he stood to make a fortune from what folks were beginning to call the New Eldorado.

Hurlan had met with his partners in Denver, telling them, "There's nothing to stop us. We'll have the best claims on the best ore lodes in the mountains. If you'll throw in with me, I'll see to it that we own the future of Colorado."

Hurlan's partners had invested under the assumption that he owned the majority of the claims on the east side of Gregory Hill. They didn't know that the

Molly Jordan was located in the middle of his holdings.

Hurlan wanted the Molly Jordan, one way or the other. The quickest and easiest way was to get rid of Devlin and McCann. Then there would be no one around to question his rights.

That was one reason why he was now so nervous. He had already spent time and money on the Molly Jordan property, blasting a shaft into the mountain and linking it with his own underground workings.

Now he had to be rid of Devlin and McCann. Otherwise, they could step onto their property and take over the workings, no questions asked.

For the past two days, Hurlan had refused visitors or guests. He had made it clear that he wanted to see no one, unless he brought a wire or a message from the men he had sent south on business.

This was not an unusual demand for Hurlan to make. He was considered quite eccentric. His help had become used to the most outlandish of requests.

Hurlan had never married and had no desire to, sharing his huge mansion with nobody. He even kept his help at separate quarters during the late evening and nighttime hours. They stayed with him only because he paid them much better than anyone else in the gulch.

Even in childhood, Marvin Hurlan had never wanted for anything. As an only child, his parents had provided well for him.

Upon their deaths, he had gained considerable wealth. He always ate the best meals money could buy, keeping his girth quite wide, and he drank the finest liquors, bourbons, and wines. He could have any woman of his choosing whenever he desired, but instead insisted on younger women exclusively, always brought to him in chains.

The third floor of his mansion was maintained for these young women. They were brought to him in pairs, new ones every other week. He would keep them for three or four days and have them taken back to a brothel in Denver that catered to his peculiar desires.

It was a very well kept secret. Lon Carlton, the younger of the two Carlton brothers, was the only one involved, besides the madam at the Denver brothel. Carlton would deliver the women, and take them back, upon demand.

For some odd reason that Hurlan couldn't understand, the madam at the brothel trusted Carlton. She had told Hurlan in no uncertain terms that she didn't want anyone else taking her girls back and forth over Smith Hill to Central City.

Along with wondering about Devlin and McCann, Hurlan's irritation also stemmed from being without a chained woman for some time. Lon Carlton had been gone longer than anticipated. He should have been back by now.

As Hurlan stared out the window, there came a knock at his door. He yelled, "It's open," and received a telegraph from a delivery boy.

The nervous servant left with a bow. Hurlan opened the envelope and read:

Problems. Serious. Will fill you in when I arrive back.

It had been signed by Lon Carlton.

The wire was far too brief for Hurlan's taste. Serious problems. He had been afraid of that.

As Hurlan reread the telegraph, he found it interesting. Carlton mentioned that they would talk about the problems when *he* got back to Central City. What did he mean by that? Was Lon Carlton the only one coming back?

It bothered Hurlan greatly that things hadn't been taken care of. Now it put undue pressure on him to get going on legal action to have the Molly Jordan mined from his own property.

Hurlan had considered it before and now wished he had progressed with the idea. He believed he could use the apex law, the common law of lode mining. This stated that an ore vein that outcropped, or apexed, on one claim could be legally mined underground into an adjacent claim.

If a vein that apexed on his property ran down beneath the Molly Jordan, Hurlan would sue to insure that he mined the underground ore.

Hurlan was flooded with anger. He mashed his cigar into an ashtray and lit another. Now he was going to have to bring in geologists and all kinds of experts, just to take the Molly Jordan. It shouldn't have to be that complicated. He had a few questions for Lon Carlton when he returned.

Hurlan read the telegram again. He tossed it out and watched it float to the floor. Why couldn't three men who had done similar jobs take care of this one, the most important one they had ever had to do?

Hurlan stared at the telegram, lying faceup on the floor. With a round of curses, he stepped over and twisted it to pieces with the heel of his boot, twisting hard as he thought about his upcoming discussion with Lon Carlton.

Sixteen

The column of wagons had circled along a little stream. The sun was falling and McCann could hear fiddle music echoing out across the vast open.

"What's that tune?" Devlin asked. "It sounds like 'Irish Washerwoman.'"

"It is," Martha said with a laugh. "That has to be Hugh Grady. He plays that tune endlessly."

"Then we must have found your people," McCann told Martha. They drew closer and the wagons could be seen plainly, some with festive markings.

Martha was already rejoicing. "Yes! Yes, it's them! There's Carl Franz's striped wagon cover. And my friend Jenny's blue water barrel."

Some of the men had already spotted them, pointing from among the wagons. The scout came out with the wagon boss and two others. He carried an old Hawken rifle.

McCann made sign language. *This looks like a good place to get a hot meal. Got any fat buffalo ribs?*

The scout laughed. He could tell that McCann knew he had once been a mountain man.

I'd give you a piece of back fat if I thought you were old enough to chew it, the scout said back in sign.

McCann laughed as well. They shook hands and, during the ride back to camp, exchanged stories about their lives among the Indians.

The scout had once been married to an Oglala Sioux woman, who had borne him two sons and had died of smallpox.

"I've never touched a trade blanket since then," the scout said. "She got the pox off'n a damned trade blanket."

In camp, Martha found her friend Jenny. With Jenny was Martha's son, Matt, who came running to her with open arms.

"Mother! You found us! I thought you'd gotten lost."

"We're alive and safe," Martha said, hugging him tightly. "That's what counts."

"Tell me what happened," Matt insisted. "Tell me what took you so long. And who are these men? Especially that one in the funny red hat."

"I'll tell you all about it later, when it's time for bed," Martha said. "But I can introduce you. This is Mr. McCann and Mr. Devlin."

The boy walked over to McCann and extended his hand. "Glad to know you, Mr. McCann. That's a big gun you're wearing. Can you shoot it real good?"

"I shoot it when I need to, Matt," McCann said. "It's good to meet you."

McCann studied the boy, just past four. Tall for his age, Matt had a bright smile and a keen sense of interest in both McCann and Devlin, who winked at him and told him they had fought Indians all the way out.

"Did you wear that red hat when you were fighting them?" Matt asked.

"I sure did," Devlin replied. "This hat brought me darned good luck, it did."

"You didn't fight no Indians," Matt said. "Old Mr. Thomas, our scout, says the Indians won't come out here as much now, since there's been a big fight with the army not long past."

Devlin was disappointed at not being able to tell a tall tale. "Maybe we ran into renegades," he told Matt. "How do you know we didn't?"

"Because if you did," Matt said, "they would have taken your red hat, and maybe what's left of your hair, too."

Devlin laughed and placed the derby on Matt's head. The derby sank down over his eyes and he danced around the fire to the fiddle music.

Jenny Prescott, Martha's good friend, served them a meal of biscuits and antelope stew. They ate heartily, talking of the ride over Raton Pass. Jenny had suspected that something was wrong, but didn't want to think that any harm had befallen Martha.

"I prayed an awful lot," she told Martha. "I knew that with just a little help from above, you'd make it through."

McCann asked about his wife and son. None of

those with the wagons had seen them, though they all said that they could easily be up ahead. Wagon trains and stagecoaches were common on the road.

McCann became uneasy again. As soon as it was light, he wanted to ride ahead and begin his search.

As the fire at Jenny's wagon cooled down to coals, McCann sat and contemplated his ride north. He would follow the main road, checking with each wagon train along the way, asking about his wife and son. Surely he would find them in the next couple of days.

Martha, sensing his nervousness, sat down next to him. She had just put Matt to bed and would join him very shortly. She hadn't slept next to her son in a long time, and she was counting her blessings.

"I suppose you're going to get an early start," she said to McCann.

"Before daybreak," McCann told her. "There's a lot of country up ahead."

"Maybe you'll find your family tomorrow," she told McCann. "They can't be that far ahead of you. You might even catch them by noon."

"I would be mighty lucky to do that," McCann said. "There's nothing to say they even took this road, or that they're even in a wagon. If they're on horseback, they would make a lot better time."

"It would be much easier to travel in a wagon," Martha said.

"You do pretty well on a horse," McCann said. "So does Minnie. She can ride better than I can."

"You think a lot of her, don't you?" Martha said. "That's admirable in a man. Very admirable."

"They don't make many like her." McCann looked at Martha. "Just a handful here and there."

Martha smiled and rose to her feet. "I'll be going

Colorado Gold

on to bed. I wish you the very best of luck in finding your wife. And I want to thank you for bringing me news about my father and mother."

"I can't thank you enough for springing us from jail," McCann said. "I hope you find your husband and that he's struck it rich."

"We'll all hold on to our dreams, won't we?" Martha said. She turned and became a shadow among the wagons.

McCann left the coals and went to the horses. He led them in and picketed them close to his and Devlin's bedrolls, for quick saddling in the morning.

As he settled in, Devlin sat up.

"Can we sleep past sunup tomorrow?" he asked.

"Of course not," McCann said. "Why would you want to waste that time?"

"We can't go on like this without rest," Devlin said. "You know where your family's headed. We'll find them, don't you worry."

"I can't rest until I've found them for certain," McCann said. "Would you be able to, if you were in my position?"

"I reckon not, lad," Devlin admitted. "But when we get to Central City, you leave me to sleep for a week, if I care to. You hear, lad?"

"Corky, when we get to Central City, you won't be able to sleep. The gold will keep you awake."

"Ah, but you know me well, don't you?" Devlin said. "I guess I'd best get my rest along the trail, while I can." He settled back down into his bedroll and was soon snoring.

McCann looked into the vast black sky and saw a star fall, blazing quickly into nothing. As he continued to watch the heavens, he was reminded of how hard it was to find someone in this huge country. It was like traveling through the mass of stars, never knowing when one might burn out next.

But he knew Minnie and his son would survive. They wouldn't burn out. He just hoped he found them before he had to deal with Carlton again.

Seventeen

Lon Carlton watched the campfire from a distance. A man and a redheaded woman sat near the flames, with a small boy beside her, eating.

Carlton had been following them since late afternoon, along with two other men, watching them closely from a distance with his spyglass. It was his way of finding likely targets for robbery.

He didn't know what to do with himself now. At Pueblo, Carlton had sent a cryptic telegram to Marvin Hurlan. He had only hinted at the failure of the mission to get Devlin and McCann. But he was certain that Hurlan understood what had happened.

The more he had thought about it, the more Carlton realized that Hurlan would be enraged. Carlton wondered if Hurlan wouldn't feel better if he brought him a present of some kind.

But the idea had made him concerned. It had

been some time since he'd been involved in any jobs. It didn't feel the same without his brother, but he knew he would have to get used to it. Nothing would be the same without Len. Nothing.

After McCann had shot Ruz, Carlton had ridden down and around, getting back on the trail well past Raton Pass. He had ridden all night and all the next day, just to be sure he had gotten far enough ahead of McCann that he wouldn't run into him somewhere.

After getting some much-needed rest, he had decided that he would pull a job on his own. He would set it up and he would pull it off, something he had never done before. He would take something for Hurlan, and that would help with things when he got back to Central City.

Carlton felt good about the idea. Maybe he could learn to do things on his own. Hurlan would see this and have more confidence in him. Maybe this would be a good way to begin.

The roads and trails were full of travelers. Some were going to Pike's Peak and vicinity, others headed farther north to Denver and up into the mountains to the west.

There were stagecoaches and freight wagons everywhere. But they were too well guarded. It would be better to choose a small group of travelers on horseback.

As Carlton watched the husband and his family, he thought about jumping them right away. That wouldn't do. There were two others who had just left to go hunting.

He had seen them checking their rifles, pointing back to a herd of deer they had passed not long before. They would hear the shots and come hurrying back.

On the other hand, if he shot the two hunters first, the man and his wife would think nothing of the gunfire.

Carlton decided to go after the hunters, get them, and hurry back. After riding less than a mile, he heard two gunshots.

He rode slowly, dismounting under the brow of a timbered hill. After tying his horse, he crept over the top.

Near the bottom of the hill, at the edge of the timber, the two hunters were dressing out a large mule deer buck with their skinning knives. Carlton eased down the slope, his rifle ready.

He could hear the men talking and laughing, happy to have the meat. They had no idea that he was there.

Carlton stuck to the timber, sneaking to within fifteen feet of the men. The late evening was on his side, offering deep shadows in the timber to hide him.

Incredible! They still had no idea that they were being watched.

Carlton found an opening that gave him a clear shot at the two men. They were so intent on their work. It would be too easy.

He pulled back the hammer on his Henry rifle and drew down on the man to his left. His back was big and broad.

Carlton touched off. The hunter arched his back and fell forward over the deer.

Panicked, Carlton quickly levered in another round. He ran from the trees toward the second man, who was turned, his eyes wide with shock.

"No!" he said, raising his hands. "No, don't shoot. Please!"

Carlton shot from his hip, hitting the man flush in the face.

Breathing heavily, Carlton looked around. No one in sight. He pulled the first man off the deer and checked his breast pocket. After all, he had been watching the man over the length of the afternoon through his spyglass.

Carlton pulled a gold watch from the dead man's pocket. He tossed it up and down in his hand a few times, smiling. Hurlan would like it a lot.

He took what cash the men had on them and rummaged through their saddlebags. In one bag he found a leather purse filled with cash. He counted nearly three hundred dollars.

Carlton felt content. With the gold watch and the cash, he had made a good haul for just two men. Now it was time to return to the husband and the redhead.

Carlton settled in to watch the husband and the redhead. They were seated at the campfire, arguing. Carlton knew they were discussing the other two men and why they hadn't returned.

Ordinarily, Carlton would have left. He didn't think either of them had many valuables, not the way they were dressed. But more baggage belonging to the two hunters now sat with them in camp. There might be more watches or cash in the bags.

Carlton wanted the man and woman to stop their arguing and climb into their bedrolls. That would make it easy for him.

More likely, the man would talk the woman into turning in, and then he would go looking for their two companions.

Carlton knew that he could shoot the man as he

Colorado Gold 141

left camp, but that would alert the woman and probably set her to screaming. He had shot screaming women before, but it hadn't been as easy as when they were sleeping or weren't expecting it.

Carlton watched awhile longer. He thought about just going into camp and getting the drop on them. It had been simple with the hunters.

But these people were already on edge and would be alert for sounds and movement. He didn't want to take the chance that the man had a gun somewhere and might be able to use it.

Still, Carlton knew that he was going to have to do something soon. If someone else came along, there could be trouble. He didn't want to leave without looking into those other bags.

Finally the woman put the boy to bed. The husband got up and took a rifle from a scabbard and checked it. The woman watched him from her bedroll. She hadn't wanted to, but she had consented to his going.

It wouldn't be as easy this way, Carlton thought. He would have to do away with the woman and the boy, then deal with the husband upon his return. He had never before faced a man coming ahead toward him. It would be something different.

As the man mounted his horse and left, Carlton began to get a strange feeling inside him. He knew that he had to kill the woman and the boy, but maybe he could have some time with her before she died.

It would be a risk, having his way before the husband returned. It was something he had never tried. It made him feel strange, and scared in a funny sort of way.

He would have to kill the boy first, though, and then shoot her quickly. He would have to be careful and not kill her with the first shot. But he would have to wound her bad enough that she didn't yell and scream.

Carlton planned the event, deciding he would muffle his shots with his saddle blanket. He didn't want the husband hearing shots and returning too quickly.

As the husband rode from camp, Carlton checked his rifle and pistol. He always preferred to use the rifle, to shoot at a distance. But in this case he would have to sneak up close. That, too, would be something different for him.

Carlton felt the pistol in his hand. He wondered how a man like Joel McCann got so good at using one. As he turned the pistol over and over, he thought how a man had to get close to make sure the job was done. That took courage and strength.

Carlton gripped the pistol. Now he would have the same power. He let the strange excitement mount. He was taking a chance, the biggest chance of his life.

Then, for an instant, he wanted to forget the whole idea. But he had spent this much time already, and the bags filled with goods were sitting right beside the woman. Besides, here was an opportunity to be strong.

Carlton checked the gold watch. The husband had been gone for ten minutes. That was enough time.

The fire was still flickering slightly, almost down to coals. His heart pounding, Carlton eased his way through the shadows, his pistol under his saddle blanket. With deliberate steps, he made his way toward the boy.

Nearly to the boy, Carlton cocked his pistol. The woman turned in her bedroll.

Carlton froze. He stared at her, trying not to breathe. Then her head came up.

"Who's there?" she said. "Who is it?"

Carlton pulled the gun up, free of the saddle blanket, and fired. The bullet ripped dirt in front of the woman's face. She sat up and screamed.

The boy lurched from his bedroll, yelling, "Mom! Run, Mom!"

Carlton turned the pistol on the boy. The woman jumped from her bedroll toward him.

Carlton turned the pistol, the woman nearly upon him, and fired point-blank into the woman's chest. She fell backward and lay still. The boy turned and began running into the shadows.

With his breath caught in his throat, Carlton emptied the pistol into the darkness after the boy. When the hammer hit on an empty chamber, he panicked.

From somewhere in the darkness nearby came a yell. "You, there! Stop!"

Running for his horse was all that Carlton could think of. Terror seized him. The bags of goods never crossed his mind. All he could think of was escape.

He heard a rifle shot and a bullet whizzed over his head. He wanted to yell like a small boy. The feeling was terrible. Another shot, and another bullet thudded into a pine near him. He did yell, feeling tears coming from his eyes.

Once on his horse, Carlton rode through the darkness as fast as his horse could carry him. There was more yelling and a few more shots, but he rode without thinking, without knowing which direction he was going, only that he didn't want anyone ever to shoot at him again. Not ever.

Eighteen

McCann led the way through the dawn, Devlin riding right behind him, protesting. "What have you got against sleep, lad? Why don't you let a man rest?"

McCann had given him the choice of staying in bed and catching up later. Devlin had decided to rise and go along instead of looking for McCann later up the trail. It wasn't a fair choice, Devlin had argued.

"How do you figure I could ever find you? You'd be riding day and night. There would be no chance a-tall, lad."

"You don't have to worry about it, Corky," McCann said. "You're here with me now. Quit complaining."

"You'd leave me and take all the gold for yourself, wouldn't you, lad?" Devlin continued. "Fine

Colorado Gold   145

way to be, I'd say. Can't see how you can look at yourself in the mirror."

McCann decided to pay him no mind. Devlin hadn't changed in the years since he'd last seen him. He would only get saltier with age.

Just after noon they met with a line of wagons whose scout told them that a woman and three men had ridden past them the day before.

"The woman, I'd say, is the one you just described," the scout said. "Small and redheaded. And yes, she had a youngster with her, a small boy. She had him riding in front of her. He sat right pert in the saddle, he did."

"Did they say where they were headed?" McCann asked.

"Denver," the scout replied. "There's gold diggings up there coming alive again, they say. The mountains above Denver is where they were headed."

"Maybe even Central City," Devlin said. "Wouldn't that be grand?" He slapped McCann on the shoulder.

Highly encouraged, McCann and Devlin rode ahead without stopping to eat. In midafternoon they came upon a camp where a man was digging a grave, shoveling the dirt as if in a trance.

Nearby, a body lay wrapped in a blanket, and a small boy knelt beside it, rocking back and forth.

Four men stood beside the grave, watching solemnly.

The four were short, stout men with strongly developed upper bodies. Their arms and shoulders were large, their chests like barrels.

The wore loose-fitting cottons and heavy felt hats, the brims upturned and stiffened with linseed oil.

"Those four men look to be Cornish, they do," Devlin commented. "Those hats, they use them in the mines, to hold candles and protect some against rocks. Best miners the old country ever saw. I wonder what's happened here."

Two of the Cornish miners were unarmed. The two who were drew their guns. McCann and Devlin, with their hands up, assured them they meant no harm.

" 'Ee's had some time of it," one of the Cornish said. He was the largest of the four, and the oldest. He pointed to the man in the grave. "Attacked by a bleddy thief, they were. She's gone. Once pretty a redhead as ever there was, I'd bet."

"A redhead?" McCann said. His stomach tightened.

"That she was," the miner said. "We found her 'usband a-digging. 'Ee showed us two of 'is friends back off the trail a piece. One shot in the back, the other in the bleddy face. Likely by the same bloke."

"Who's the man digging?" McCann asked.

" 'Ee's the 'usband, and won't let us 'elp 'im dig. 'Ee's set to grieving in an odd sort of way. When I told 'im I'd 'elp 'im bury 'er, whether or not, 'ee near to knocked me head off with the bleddy shovel."

"You'd do best to just ride on," another miner said.

"Shortly," McCann said. He dismounted, his stomach in knots, and walked to the grave.

"It's best to leave 'im be," the big miner warned.

"I need to talk to him," McCann said.

" 'Ee's not one for that."

McCann stood at the edge of the grave. "I'm sorry, mister," he said, "but I need to talk to you."

Colorado Gold

The husband ignored him and continued digging.

"I need to look at the woman," McCann said, "if you'll let me."

The husband looked up from his digging. "What?"

"I need to see her," McCann said.

"Do I know you?"

"No. My partner and I just rode in."

"You'd as well ride out. I don't want no help from anyone. Just let me dig in peace."

"I've been looking for my wife," McCann explained. "I heard she was on her way up this trail. What was her name?"

"I just called her Red."

McCann held his breath. "Was her real name Minnie?"

"Why all the questions?"

"I've been looking for my wife since the end of the war. She's small and redheaded. Was her real name Minnie?"

"I don't know. I just called her Red." He began digging again.

"How long were you married to her?" McCann asked.

"Six months," the man said. "She said she lost her husband in the war."

Two miners approached McCann. "It's time to leave," one of them said.

"Listen, I need to know about this," McCann said.

"No, it's best you'd go on your way."

Devlin stood behind them, his rifle leveled. "He's not about to hurt anyone. He's worried his own self. He just wants to know."

The man in the grave dug without paying any attention.

"We'll shoot 'im," one of the men told Devlin. "We'll fill 'im with bleddy 'oles,"

"And I'll get you," Devlin said. "By all that's holy, I'll drop as many as I can, I will."

The big Cornish turned to the others. "I'd say they mean no 'arm to anyone. Leave 'em bleddy be."

McCann looked into the grave. His stomach twisted harder. "Can I look at her? I've got to see her. If you were me, wouldn't you want to know?"

"I suppose," the man said. "Go ahead. I don't mind."

Devlin put a hand on McCann's shoulder. "You sure you want to do this, lad?"

"I have to, Corky."

"I reckon you do, at that. Just take your time."

McCann approached the body. He felt sick. His heart was hammering within, and sweat beaded on his brow.

The boy was still kneeling on the ground, slumped over, his head down. He said nothing, but rocked himself back and forth.

"What's your name?" McCann asked him. He got no reply. The boy was not talking.

McCann took a deep breath and pulled the blanket back. The woman lay calm in death, her face pale, her eyes closed. There was a neat round hole in her blouse, just above her left breast.

McCann let his breath out. It was not Minnie.

The woman could easily have passed for her sister, almost her twin. But it was not Minnie.

McCann realized he was shaking. He laid the

blanket back over the woman and struggled to his feet.

"You all right, lad?" Devlin asked.

McCann steadied himself. "That's not Minnie. I'm sorry for what's happened here, but thank God, that's not Minnie."

"She has to be the woman we've been following, and her son. Don't you think?"

"No doubt," McCann said. "But it wasn't Minnie. I wonder where Minnie is, and if she's dead."

"You can't know that, lad. And you can't dwell on it. The good Lord has His ways and we can't figure them, no we can't."

McCann had heard Devlin say that or words similar many times, especially during the war. Battles would turn one way or the other under strange circumstances. "The Lord's at work and we've but to trust in His ways," Devlin would say.

His hope shattered, McCann stared at the blanket and then at the man digging. He had been sure he was following Minnie. But it hadn't been her, and the feeling was very odd.

He thought about the boy and turned. Still hunched over, still silent, the boy seemed ready to collapse. McCann went over and knelt to take him in his arms.

At first the boy resisted. But McCann talked in a low tone and the boy fell into his chest, sobbing loudly. McCann wondered if anyone had had to take care of his own son in the same way, somewhere far away, on some forgotten trail. The thought shook him to the depths of his soul.

The dead woman's husband climbed out of the grave. He stood near McCann and the boy.

"My name's Malone," he told McCann. "I aim to

take care of him as best I can. He'll be with me in Denver and thereabouts. I figure to make good in the gold fields and send him to a proper school."

"I hope you can," McCann said. "He's a fine boy."

The boy went to Malone and stood beside him, staring at the blanket.

"He won't forget this day, he won't," Devlin said. "Never will he forget it."

The Cornish miners gathered around McCann and Devlin. "We'll be apologizing for trying to send you away," the big one said. "It was poor of us and we regret it."

"It's understandable," McCann said. "After what's happened here, I could believe you might have shot at us."

"I hope you find your dear wife and son," the miner said. "It's a 'ard place to be, out 'ere in and away from it all."

"Did anyone ever see the thief?" Devlin asked.

"No, none of us. But the 'usband did, as the thief took to 'is 'orse. Now look at 'im. God bless 'is poor soul, 'ee don't know if it's day or night."

McCann and Devlin stayed for the burial, offering to help fill in the grave. The husband still wanted no help. But he was willing to travel with the Cornish miners on to Denver.

"And we'd 'ave you both with us as well," the big miner told McCann. "You did, by God, a good turn by 'at boy just now. My name's Eaden Penrose." He pointed to the other men. "That be my brother, Boddy, who speaks not a bleddy word. And those two would be Arlin Trewain and Gorwain Polweal. We'd be 'appy to 'ave ye as bleddy friends."

Devlin, particularly, was happy for the invitation.

He had hoped to line up Cornish miners to help them get their mine going. By chance they had already found some; and if these men didn't already have a mine to work, there might be a good chance of making a deal.

They rode mostly in silence, in respect for the husband and the boy. The boy kept looking back. He hadn't wanted to leave the grave site, but realized after McCann talked to him that staying would not bring his mother back.

It haunted McCann to see the boy. He wondered over and over if his wife and son were safe or gone. As Devlin had pointed out, he couldn't know and didn't have any way of finding out unless he got another lead somewhere.

After what had just happened, McCann worried about getting another lead. He wasn't certain if he could go through what he just had again, especially if the woman who had been killed turned out to be Minnie.

He decided to turn his interests toward the mine and, for the time being, forget about trying to locate his wife and son. If he heard something about a redheaded woman, he would see what he could find out. Otherwise, He would help Devlin with the Molly Jordan.

As they camped for the night, it appeared more and more that Eaden Penrose and the other Cornish miners would be willing to work for Devlin and McCann, for a percentage of the profits. The men seemed to know everything about underground mining and how to do the work most efficiently.

"Can you believe it, lad?" Devlin asked McCann. "They fell right into our pocket. You couldn't ask for better. You couldn't."

"They don't know about our problems yet," McCann pointed out. "They don't know about Carlton and Marvin Hurlan. That might change their minds."

"No, I don't figure that will stop them. They'll want in with us for sure, once we tell them how it is with Hurlan. They'll know for sure that Molly Jordan's a good claim."

McCann called Penrose and the others over to the fire and explained their problem. They all listened intently. Penrose called the others together, and after a short time, he returned.

"We've decided, to a man, to fall in with ye, if the offer still 'olds. We've decided you both be fit men to work for."

"Then that's it," Devlin said with a smile. "As soon as we find ourselves a bottle, we'll drink to it, we will."

"Aye, drink to it, we will," Penrose said with a laugh. "There's not a man alive can stop us from bringing the lode out of the Molly Jordan."

Nineteen

Marvin Hurlan was seated at his desk when one of the servants knocked on the door.

"What is it?" Hurlan yelled.

The door opened. "Mr. Carlton to see you. Mr. Lon Carlton."

"Show him in."

Carlton stepped into the office. The servant closed the door and Hurlan rose from his desk, smoke pouring from the cigar in his mouth. He picked up the soiled and tattered telegram and walked around his desk.

"Well, Carlton. I see by your wire that things have gone bad."

"First, before we talk about anything," Carlton said, "I brought you a present." He pulled the gold watch from his pocket and handed it to Hurlan.

Hurlan took the watch and studied it. "What's

this for? Do you want me to like you or something?"

"No. It's a present. For you."

Hurlan dropped the watch at his feet and slammed his bootheel into it. Fragments skittered all over the floor.

"What did you do that for?" Carlton asked.

"I didn't ask for any presents. I asked you to do a job. Now, what happened?"

Carlton was staring at the shattered gold watch. He bent over and retrieved it, putting the remains in his pocket. "It didn't happen the way we wanted it," he said to Hurlan angrily.

Hurlan met his glare, his cigar aglow. "So why not?"

Carlton worked to compose himself. "McCann, Devlin's partner, is a gunfighter. We didn't expect that."

"A gunfighter? Devlin's no gunfighter."

"I didn't say Devlin. I said his partner. McCann, his partner." Saying it made Carlton feel odd. In his mind he was back in Carminga. He could see McCann pumping bullets into his brother, and his brother falling.

Hurlan walked behind his desk and began pacing, his cigar bellowing smoke. "You and your brother have gone against gunmen before. Why's this McCann so different?"

"He got the drop on us in Carminga," Carlton lied. "He must have known about us. He came into the saloon and opened fire. I was lucky to get away."

Hurlan stopped his pacing and studied Carlton. "You were the only one to get away? DuCain and your brother were both killed, and you got away?"

"I was fast enough to get around the bar, under cover," Carlton replied. "I shot at him and I think I wounded him. He ducked outside, and I left out the back."

"If you wounded him," Hurlan asked, "then why didn't you stay and finish the job?"

Carlton shuffled his feet. "I couldn't find him. I looked. He must have been hiding in the trees or something."

"Where was Devlin?"

"Devlin?"

"Oh, come on! Where was Devlin while this was going on? Surely he should have been there."

"No, he hadn't arrived yet." Carlton was thinking as fast as he could. "McCann got there first and got the jump on us. I left before Devlin got to town."

"That's interesting," Hurlan said. He picked up clippings from Cimarron and Sante Fe newspapers that he had received in the mail that morning. "I've got some stories here that talk about Hank Trent being shot by some big gunman, who had a partner with a red derby hat. Who would those two be?"

Carlton was trapped. "I tried to get Hank Trent to help me. He and Chico Ruz took them to jail. But a blond woman broke them out."

"A blond woman named Martha Jacobson. Right?"

"Yeah, that's her."

"You see," Hurlan said, glaring at Carlton, "I have friends in different places. They look after me. I'll learn what's going on whether or not you tell me the truth."

"I didn't know what to do," Carlton said. "I thought Hank Trent and Chico Ruz could help me."

"Well, you haven't done me any favors, Carlton. They're putting a federal marshal on the case."

"They are? Isn't that good?"

Hurlan chomped his cigar in rage. "Think about it, Carlton. If they catch McCann, he'll tell his side of the story, and he'll get Martha Jacobson to talk, also. I hope you know that her husband is a well-respected lawyer. He used to work for Lucien Maxwell in Cimarron."

"I heard that," Carlton said.

"Then you know that the woman's husband is looking into mining and setting up his law practice in Denver. He's getting to be well known around here. If he gets into it, there very well could be an investigation into Hank Trent and Chico Ruz. That investigation could lead back to me. I wish you hadn't brought them into it."

"I thought for sure we could get them," Carlton said. "We went after them, and Ruz knew the country. But McCann shot everyone."

"This McCann fellow, he must be a very tough one."

"No, he's mostly a coward," Carlton said quickly. "He shoots folks in the back, when they're not looking."

"Whatever he does, he's put us in a bind," Hurlan said. "When he and Devlin arrive, they can go right up to that mine and start working it, and I can't do a thing about it. Not until I go through a lot of legal maneuvers. That takes time, Carlton, and I don't want my investors knowing that someone owns a claim right in the middle of my property. I don't want them thinking that I lied to them. Do you understand, Carlton?"

"I'll figure something out," Carlton said. "I can get the job done."

"How? You couldn't before. And you had a lot of help. Your brother, Len, did most of the work for me. Not you. I can't imagine how he could have gotten himself killed. DuCain is another story. He's a better brawler than a shooter. But your brother, he was much more careful than that."

"It hurts that he's gone," Carlton said. "I can't hardly believe it."

"He was just another shooter," Hurlan said. "He shouldn't have been so stupid."

"He wasn't stupid!" Carlton was seething. "How could you say that? I told you, McCann got the jump on us. He's a coward."

"None of that matters now," Hurlan said. "There are a lot of problems, and I've got to go through a lot of legal wrangling to get the job done. I wanted to avoid that."

"What if you lose in court?" Carlton asked.

"I don't intend to!" Hurlan barked. "That's what I'm talking about. It will be costly, and they will be mining that claim all the while. Besides, I told you, I don't want my investors involved."

"Maybe you shouldn't have opened a shaft," Carlton suggested. "Maybe you should have waited."

Hurlan came around the desk, pointing his finger at Carlton. "Now, you listen to me. If you'd done your job, there wouldn't be any problems to consider. I don't want to hear any more from you. In fact, I'm not certain if I need you any longer."

"Why wouldn't you need me?"

"Because you can't get a job done, that's why."

Carlton stared at Hurlan. "Then I guess you'll

lose your connections with Old Lady Sawyer down in Denver."

Hurlans's eyes narrowed. "What do you mean by that?"

"Who else is going to arrange for your girls? Who's going to bring them up here for you? The old lady likes me, you know. You can't get them that young from anybody else."

"I'll find somebody else to take your place," Hurlan said. "It won't be that hard."

"Don't be so sure," Carlton said. "It'll take time. You know how hard it was to get the old lady to trust me. She won't like having to break in somebody new."

Hurlan puffed on his cigar. He walked to the window and peered out. A large group was on its way up the street to Lemkuhl's Brewery for a party in the garden. Hurlan was scheduled to host such a party the following week, when his partners came in for their monthly meeting.

Hurlan wanted everything taken care of by then. He didn't want any loose ends to stall his plans, or cause any of his investors to have second thoughts.

Carlton couldn't be of much help, Hurlan thought. He was a coward and looked for the easy way of getting things done. But Carlton had him in a bind if he wanted to continue getting girls from Old Lady Sawyer's brothel.

Carlton, the little swine, was right. Old Lady Sawyer filled his wishes, for a very good price, and wouldn't like any change of plans. For some reason, she let Carlton come and go when she wouldn't most anyone else.

Hurlan knew that to try and change things would take time. It would take away from his efforts to get

Colorado Gold

rid of Devlin and McCann. And it would keep him from having the girls when he wanted them.

That was most important. Now, in this time of stress, he needed the girls. Carlton would have to stay—for the time being.

Hurlan turned back from the window. "You can stay on, Carlton. But I'm going to have to get you some help with Devlin and McCann. You can't do it all alone."

"I can do it."

"Think about it, Carlton. If three of you went to Carminga and only you survived, and then both Trent and Ruz went down, how do you expect to finish things alone?"

"What do you want to do?" Carlton asked.

"I'm going to hire a man that one of my friends told me about. He used to lead guerilla raids along the Kansas and Missouri borders during the war. He'll help you."

"You mean a Jayhawker?"

"I don't care what you call him. He comes highly recommended. I've already got a job lined up for him."

"I'll be the boss, though. Right?"

"You'll work together, Carlton. You'll be equals."

"I don't know if I like that."

"You don't have a choice, Carlton."

Carlton's face turned red. He thought about quitting Hurlan, telling him right then and there. Then Hurlan wouldn't know what to do. Especially since he wouldn't have anyone Old Lady Sawyer trusted to run her girls back and forth to Hurlan.

But he could see Hurlan studying him, daring him. Carlton knew that if he quit, or even threatened to, Hurlan would have him killed, probably by the Jayhawker he was bringing in.

Carlton thought better of pushing Hurlan further. Hurlan was already enraged. To say something more would push Hurlan too far. When you pushed Marvin Hurlan too far, he got crazy. And he always managed to cover up what he'd done.

"What's this Jayhawker's name?" Carlton asked.

"You'll know when he gets here."

"When do you expect him?"

"I'll send for you when he arrives."

"That's real good, Mr. Hurlan. That will be just fine. I'll be waiting, then."

"In the meantime, Carlton, I want you to make a trip to Denver for me. You know how to handle it. Be back tonight. Make sure the girls are drugged."

"I know all of that, Mr. Hurlan."

Hurlan took a deep breath and blew cigar smoke toward the window. "Good. You can go now. I'll let you know when the other man arrives. He'll stop in Denver for a bit and then come up here. I want our problems cleared up right away."

"You don't have to worry, Mr. Hurlan. Our problems *will* be cleared up right away."

Carlton eased the team of mules down Smith Hill Road through the late afternoon sunlight. He was driving a small freight wagon, the kind he always used to pick up the girls in Denver. It was loaded with a few goods, covered by canvas. When it got dark, the drugged girls would be laid among the freight boxes and taken back up the hill.

As Carlton drove, he thought about his meeting with Hurlan. It had bothered him that Hurlan hadn't cared about Len's death. Hurlan hadn't shown that

Colorado Gold

he even knew Len all that well, except to say that he was careful on his jobs and that he couldn't understand how Len had gotten himself shot.

Hurlan had known Len very well. DuCain, he hadn't known all that well, nor Trent or Chico Ruz. But Len, he had known for a long time.

It bothered Carlton to think that Hurlan saw them as nothing more than servants. In fact, he treated his servants better. And after all the jobs he and Len had done for Hurlan, to dismiss Len's death so casually was enraging. It was hard to understand.

And the gold watch. Hurlan had smashed it like a piece of mud on his boots.

Carlton thought about it. Hurlan cared little for anything but getting women in chains once in a while. He made people think that he was a good businessman and wanted the best for Central City, but he didn't care about any of that. Gold and helpless women, that's all he cared for.

And now the red-hatted Devlin and his gunfighting partner were bothering Hurlan to the point that he would pay highly for a killer from the war, some Jayhawker who wanted to earn a fast poke of gold.

At the bottom of the hill, Carlton checked the action on his rifle. Smooth. He thought about how he had shot the hunters. He had done it on his own. He started to feel that strange excitement again.

If Hurlan wanted to bring someone in to get rid of Devlin and McCann, that man would have to be pretty good. He would have to be very good.

Carlton began to think that he could do just as well as any Jayhawker. He remembered how it had been to be nearly shot; but after getting away, he had gotten a jolt of excitement out of it. That must be what it was like to face a man head-on.

Carlton's mind went back to the Jayhawker. He would no doubt be in soon. Maybe within a matter of days. He wondered what the Jayhawker's business was in Denver. It didn't matter. What counted was after the Jayhawker got to Central City.

The more Carlton thought about it, the more he was sure that Hurlan was bringing him in to take care of McCann. But no, Hurlan had promised that he could have McCann. The Jayhawker was just being hired to help with other matters.

Carlton smiled and set his rifle back down on the seat. He would go into Denver and get the girls, and he would haul them back up the hill, just like always. Then he would get McCann. Before long, Marvin Hurlan would know that he could do a lot more than just be a delivery boy.

Twenty

McCann sat in Devlin's cabin on the edge of Central City, reading a local paper. He and Devlin had reached town the night before and had slept soundly, lying in bunks for the first time in a long time.

Now, at midmorning, McCann caught up on local news while Devlin lay on his bed, nursing a bottle of whiskey.

"A man never knows what he takes for granted until he's without it, eh, lad?"

McCann nodded.

"You aren't listening to me a-tall, lad," Devlin said. "I'm so happy, you know. Them Cornishmen are a godsend, they are. By week's end we'll have more help than we know what to do with."

Penrose and the others were on the streets, soliciting other Cornish miners looking for work. As soon as they had found enough recruits, they would start mining.

Devlin talked about going up to the mine and showing McCann the old claim, and how they could begin tunneling into the mountain.

"Yes, I can see it all now," Devlin was saying. "The headlines will read: MOLLY JORDAN MINE IS RICHEST IN COLORADO: Makes Corky Devlin, Adventurer, Fabulously Wealthy."

McCann nodded again. He was reading about the growth and development going on in Denver and up the gold-packed gulches. The New Eldorado, as the headlines called it, was attracting thousands from all over the country, and also from abroad.

Marvin Hurlan was mentioned as a prominent citizen of Central City, a man who was looking to the future. The article went on to say that Hurlan was planning a public library in his name, as well as a school.

McCann tossed the paper aside and rubbed his hands though his hair. Hurlan was going to be a hard man to put down.

"You look happy as a greased bear," Devlin said, sipping from his bottle. "What's ailing you, lad?"

"Hurlan's setting himself up as a pillar of the community," McCann replied. "It's going to be hard for us."

"Well, don't you worry none, lad," Devlin said. "We've got the Cornishmen on our side. They know the miners around here and they know how to do the mining. You just remember, what goes on underground is what supports what you see on top."

"I suppose so, Corky," McCann said. "Hurlan hasn't been able to have us killed outright yet, but

Colorado Gold

you can bet he's also looking into legal ways to get rid of us."

"Let him try all he can," Devlin said. "He'll not get the best of us, he won't. Not by a long shot."

There came a knock at the door. Penrose spoke from outside it. "Open up. We've come with some news you'd ought to be 'eering."

McCann opened the door and Penrose entered, with five other Cornishmen.

Devlin sat up. "You all look ready to bite nails. What's come over you?"

Penrose said, "Our Mr. 'urlan is a-mining the Molly Jordan."

"What are you saying?" Devlin asked.

"Just that," Penrose replied. "We've just come from there. 'Ee's dug a shaft and it's plain as day."

"We've got to get up there," Devlin told McCann. "He's got no right to our gold."

"Let's plan this out," McCann said.

"What's to plan?" Devlin asked. "The fiend's after our gold, and I aim to stop him."

"I'd be for listening to 'im, if I were you," Penrose told McCann. "I've got a good many who'll dig for us. I'll get them together and the lot of us will be 'eaded up there with you. The sooner the better."

McCann walked outside. Cornishmen were milling around, waiting for orders. Some of them were already mounted, ready to ride up to the mine.

"It's time we took a step forward, lad," Devlin said. "Otherwise, Hurlan will be a-stepping on us for certain."

McCann fastened his gun belt on, while Penrose and the others watched him.

"You ever shoot a man underground?" Penrose asked.

"Never have," McCann replied.

"You're in for a treat, then," Penrose said, clapping him on the back. "A real treat."

McCann and Devlin stood at the entrance to the Molly Jordan. Penrose and the Cornish miners were preparing themselves to go into the mountain.

True to Penrose's word, a shaft had been started and timbers laid. No ore had yet been taken out, but it appeared that the work could begin at any time.

"Can you believe that?" Devlin asked. "Hurlan was so certain we would be dead that he started mining our claim. The fiend!"

"We should thank him, Corky," McCann said. "He's gone to some expense to get us started here."

"That he has, lad," Devlin said. "I'll be sending him a thank-you card directly."

Penrose stepped forward. He had affixed a candle, upright, into the brim of his hat and carried a hammer and a number of steel pins. A long coil of rope rested on his stout shoulder.

"We're ready to take a look at 'er," he said. "You give the word."

The rest of the Cornishmen, ready to explore the mine, stood stoically behind Penrose.

"What do you say, lad?" Devlin asked McCann.

McCann checked his Colt. "I'm ready."

"Then let's get at it," Devlin said.

Penrose and the other Cornishmen lit their candles. McCann and Devlin both struck lanterns. Penrose led the way, with Devlin and McCann right behind. They stopped at intervals while Penrose checked the timber structure, complaining often that the construction was shoddy.

"This is stout rock, it is," he told Devlin and McCann, "but she's got to 'ave good support 'ere and there. This was done in a mighty big 'urry, without a care to the workers."

Another Cornishman remarked, "Whoever this Mr. 'urlan be, 'ee's not one to care about 'is men."

McCann asked who would have done the contruction, if not men working for Hurlan.

"It likely was miners working for 'urlan," Penrose said. "But they bleddy don't know their work. They won't be Cornish, they won't."

The tunnel ran deep into the mountain, along a visible vein. The rock had been blasted along seams, and ore crystals gleamed in the lantern light.

One of the Cornishmen came forward with a pick. Penrose chipped at the wall and pulled a piece out.

"She's a bleddy good strike, she is!" he said, studying the rock. "I'd jump into the air, was the tunnel a bit 'igher."

Devlin was so excited, he could barely hold his lantern still. "Did you ever see such a thing, lad? There's enough gold to keep me happy for, say, at least a week." He laughed and slapped McCann on the back. "All of us in here couldn't spend it in a lifetime."

A short distance farther, the tunnel took a ninety-degree turn to the left. Penrose walked into the new shaft a short distance and returned.

"If I don't miss my guess, I'd say someone's tied us into another mine nearby," he reported. "A sneaky way to be."

"So this is it," Devlin said. "Hurlan's had his

men dig across, tying our tunnel in with his property. He figures to take our ore from two directions."

"The thing of it is," Penrose pointed out, "the ore's coming from your claim. It's angled down into 'urlan's property."

"What a stroke of luck!" Devlin said. "The apex law is on our side! We can go into Hurlan's mine and take ore that's rightfully ours."

"Better'n that, we can rightfully call Mr. 'urlan's mine our own." Penrose nodded. "The vein is slanted from the top down into 'is own mine, neat as you please. I'd bet 'ee'd be for filling this in if 'ee knew the truth."

"That's likely why Hurlan dug the shaft," McCann said. "He wanted to know where the ore went. He was hoping he could use the apex law. But it backfired on him, and now we'll have the legal edge."

"That's all good and well," Penrose said. "But we've got to come down below 'ere and mine 'er, just the same. Let's see what's ahead."

"We'd best be careful, lads," Devlin warned. "Like as not, we're headed into trouble."

"We've seen trouble a time or two," Penrose said. "We've thrown in with you two and for bleddy certain we'll stick it out, through thick and thin."

They advanced cautiously, coming to an area that had seen recent work. A deep shaft had been dug and blasted straight down into the mountain.

Penrose tossed a rock over the edge. It bounced off the sides, finally splashing into water far below.

"Ah, she's a deep one," Penrose said. "Was a man to take a swim in there, 'ee'd likely have to stay a night or two."

Colorado Gold

The others laughed nervously. Then everyone was silent. They were all remembering friends in the old country, lost in mine shafts such as that one.

Penrose broke the silence. "It's so quiet. You'd think a man would 'ear picks and shovels a ways over, where Mr. 'urlan's diggings are."

The shaft extended past the deep hole, well into the mountain on Hurlan's claim, but there was no sound of miners anywhere near.

"It does seem odd, don't it?" Devlin agreed. "I'd figure Hurlan to have his men busy as bees down here."

Penrose started forward. "Let's see how much farther we can go."

Devlin stopped him. "Do you smell that?"

A sulfurous smudge began to fill the tunnel.

"Turn and run for it, lads!" Devlin yelled.

Rifle fire sounded from back in the tunnel. One of the Cornishmen grabbed his leg and slipped into the hole, yelling as he fell. The echoes died out when there was a loud *sploosh* way below.

The others scrambled toward the main tunnel, the sulfurous smell choking them. They were just rounding the corner into the new shaft when an explosion tore through the side tunnel, hurling dust and rocks through the mine.

Two of the Cornishmen yelled. McCann and Devlin hurried back with Penrose and four others. As they worked to free the miners from the rocks, more rifle fire began tearing through the shaft.

McCann pulled his Colt and shot into the darkness. He fired until his Colt was empty, keeping the return fire from the rifle at a minimum.

"We've got to do this fast," Devlin said, holding

the head of an injured miner. "If the rifle fire don't get us, the smudge will."

Finally the trapped miners were free. The others lifted them into the new tunnel and took them out to be laid in a wagon.

"We'll find a doctor, we will," Penrose told the injured men. "Don't fret none."

"I should have figured it for a trap," Devlin said. "One of Hurlan's miners was in there, just waiting to set off a blast."

"Whoever tried to get us was no miner," Penrose said. "I could set off a better blast before I was a-walking."

The other Cornishmen agreed. Their anger raged at having lost one of their own down the deep shaft.

"We'll 'ave to get 'im up from there," one of the miners said. "'Is missus will be a-grieving."

Everyone was worried about the two injured miners as well. They had both sustained broken arms and legs. One had a head injury, and the other appeared to have broken ribs. They both lay unconscious in the wagon.

"I would say that Hurlan sent Carlton to finish us off," Devlin said. "He wants to stop us before we get started."

"He's made a mess of it," McCann said. "If he'd gotten us all back there, he could say we were all killed in a mining accident. That would have been neat and convenient. He's made it hard on himself now."

" 'Ee's made us bleddy mad is what 'ee's done," Penrose said. "If it's war Mr. 'urlan wants, 'ee's sure got it."

Twenty-One

Carlton stood inside Marvin Hurlan's office, nervously squeezing his hat. Hurlan was standing behind his desk, chomping his cigar.

"What gave you the idea you could do something like that?" Hurlan asked. "You don't know anything about blasting. And shooting underground, what were you trying to do?"

"You know," Carlton said. "I was trying to get McCann. I nearly did."

"Nearly's not close enough," Hurlan said. "You didn't get him. All you've done is caused me a lot of problems. How am I going to explain all this? How am I going to tell my investors that there was an accident in the mine? They won't have a lot of faith in me."

"I just wanted Devlin and McCann," Carlton said. "I didn't figure all those miners would be with him."

"You shouldn't have tried it in the first place," Hurlan said. "Did I tell you to do it?"

"No."

"Did you bother to tell me that you were going to set them up?"

"No."

Hurlan slammed his hand flat against his desk. "Then why did you do it?"

"I told you, I wanted to get McCann."

"We all want to get McCann," Hurlan said. "But I've told you, I don't want you doing *anything* without my permission. Can you understand that?"

Carlton squeezed his hat. "I understand."

It was bad enough being dressed down, but there was a third man present in the room. The Jayhawker Hurlan had sent for had arrived that morning and was now sitting in a chair beside Hurlan's desk. He seemed amused.

His name was Jensen, and he was wearing an expensive suit. Carlton was certain the man wasn't used to suits; Hurlan had dressed him up that way to make it appear that he was a business partner.

Carlton could see that Jensen's hands and his eyes were hard as stone. There was nothing about him that was refined, except maybe the way he hunted men.

Compared to either Trent or Ruz, though, Carlton saw this man as second-rate. He didn't appear as dangerous, by far, as either of them. And McCann had killed both Trent and Ruz with relative ease.

Carlton decided that maybe together he and Jensen could get McCann.

"I'll work with Mr. Jensen here from now on," Carlton suggested. "We'll take care of McCann together."

Carlton noticed the amusement on Jensen's face. Jensen turned toward the window to hide his smile.

"Why don't you let me figure how things will be handled," Hurlan told Carlton. "I want you to do just what you've been doing: going back and forth to Denver. If I need anything else from you, I'll let you know."

"But we've got to stop McCann and Devlin before they clear out that tunnel and get to mining."

Hurlan chomped hard on his cigar. "We're wasting a lot of time here, Carlton. I want you to run a load of freight down to Denver for me. When you're getting the wagon, tell them over at the stables that Mr. Jensen will be there right away to pick up a horse. Tell them to give him the palomino."

"That's your best horse," Carlton said. "I figured someday to buy him off you."

"Maybe someday, Carlton," Hurlan said. "But for the time being, Mr. Jensen is going to use him. You can get going now."

Carlton twisted his hat and left. He rode over to the stables, thinking about Jensen. Hurlan had mentioned his name, but hadn't introduced him.

And giving him the palomino to ride was hard to believe. He'd never allowed anyone to ride that horse. He must be trying to make Jensen feel right at home.

It made Carlton wonder if Hurlan wasn't going to keep Jensen on permanently. It made him wonder further if Hurlan meant to have Jensen go after McCann by himself.

Getting used to life without his brother, Len, was going to take Carlton more time than he had thought. And bringing a new man in wasn't going to help.

Despite what had happened in the mine, Carlton was growing more determined to do things on his own. He didn't want to wait to get McCann; he wanted McCann right away. And he didn't want to wait for Hurlan's orders.

Hurlan stood in his office, watching Carlton leave. He brought Jensen to the window and pointed.

"I'm not going to have that man working for me much longer. He's gotten so that he doesn't follow orders very well."

"Why don't you just tell him to leave?" Jensen suggested.

"It's not that simple," Hurlan said. "He just lost his brother to a gunfighter, and it's cost him what little mind he had to begin with. His brother got things done for me. This one is worthless without guidance."

"I still don't see the problem," Jensen said.

Hurlan turned from the window. He led Jensen up two flights of stairs to the third floor. He opened the door to a small room and entered.

Jensen followed and stared at two young women in torn dresses, sitting on the floor in chains. Both women were droopy-eyed, as if they'd been drugged.

"I have a different sort of taste, you might say," Hurlan explained. "No matter what you might think of it, that's the way it is with me."

"I'd say this wasn't so different." Jensen was smiling. "Do you ever share?"

"We'll see," Hurlan said. "But the problem with losing Carlton is that he's the one who brings the women up here from Denver. He goes to get them, and the old lady there likes him. She's an odd one, and she's told me that Carlton is the only one she can trust with her girls."

"I'll bet I could get the old lady to liking me," Jensen said.

"That would be very good," Hurlan said. "I've got a job for you down in Denver, anyway. I would like to have you stop and see the old lady while you're there. Tell her that I sent you. See how she acts." He studied Jensen. "You know what to do."

"Like I said," Jensen said, smiling, "I think I can get her to like me way better than she does Carlton. What does she see in him, anyway?"

"He's no threat," Hurlan said. "She knows she can keep our secret with him. And she can trust him not to take the girls somewhere and kill them. It's getting harder to steal girls and keep them doped up."

Hurlan closed the door and led the way back down to his office. "This job in Denver is very important. It's to be an accident, and it has to be handled just right."

"Who is it?"

"A lawyer who can do me a great deal of damage. I don't want that. I don't know him at all, but I do know that he's very anxious to meet me. That's what will make your job that much easier."

"When do you want it done?"

"Today. He's to come up here for a business dinner. You will be his escort. Like I said, it has to be an accident."

"I'm good at accidents," Jensen said. "Real good."

Twenty-Two

Martha Jacobson got down from the wagon and ran into her husband's arms. Market Street, downtown Denver, was alive with activity. Martha cared nothing at all about what was going on around her. Being with her husband again was the best feeling she had had in a long time.

"It took you longer than I had thought," Blaine Jacobson told Martha as he pulled Matt into his arms. "I feared something had happened along the way."

"We were saved," Matt told his father.

"You were saved?"

"Yes, by a man with a red hat and a tall man with a big pistol. They were nice."

"It sounds like a lot has happened," Jacobson said to Martha.

"We've had some trying times," Martha said. "But we're all together now. That's what counts."

Martha had wired Jacobson from Pueblo, shortly after saying good-bye to McCann and Devlin. She had gotten his wire back, telling her how worried he had been when she hadn't responded to his messages sent to Cimarron. She had wired him back that he would hear the entire story when they met in Denver.

Since getting her last wire, Jacobson had received a letter from his old employer, Lucien Maxwell, with clippings from area newspapers. The articles had detailed a jailbreak by two outlaws who allegedly had been helped by a prominent woman of Cimarron named Martha Jacobson.

"You must have a lot to fill me in on, Martha," Jacobson said.

"It will take some time, Blaine," she said, stroking Matt's hair. "Let's get settled first."

"We'll go on up to the house, then," Jacobson said. "I've found us a nice place in the Cherry Creek district. A lot has been happening for me."

Martha said good-bye to her good friend Jenny and the others, who were all anxious to get on the road up the gulch to Nevada City, where other friends were awaiting their arrival. Martha wished them luck and settled with Matt into a small carriage Jacobson had brought from their new home.

The day was open and warm and the roads were filled with citizens and travelers. Martha remarked that the city was beautiful.

"A lot of growth is expected," Jacobson said. "This is already a very important community."

"That's good," Martha said. "So I take it you like it here."

"Very much."

"Have you struck it rich yet?"

"I've struck it very rich, my dear. I have you back by my side."

Martha sensed that he was saying it just for her benefit. He didn't even look at her. It bothered her, for she felt something different about him. He had changed in some way.

"How have things been going for you?" Martha asked.

Jacobson explained that he was receiving offers from prominent citizens to handle their legal affairs, including some mine owners whose holdings had already begun to pay big dividends.

"I've even got an offer to handle all legal matters for a major citizen up in Central City. His name is Marvin Hurlan, and he's invited me up to meet with him."

"That's interesting," Martha said. "What did you say his name was?"

"Marvin Hurlan. Have you heard the name?"

"As a matter of fact, I have," Martha said. She looked at Matt. "We can discuss that later as well."

"Yes, later," Jacobson said. "And at the same time, we can discuss this business in Cimarron."

"How did you know about that?" Martha asked.

"It's in all the papers, Martha. You can tell me about it."

At their home, Jacobson gave Martha a tour. It was the most beautiful Victorian mansion that she had ever seen, with three stories of spacious rooms.

"What will we do with all this?" Martha asked.

"Live in it," Jacobson replied. "After our problems are settled, we'll live happily in it."

Colorado Gold 179

Matt was standing in the doorway to his bedroom. "This is for me?"

"Why don't you try that big bed out?" Martha suggested. "This is a good afternoon for a nap."

"I think it would be good to sleep in," Matt agreed. "And I'm kind of tired."

Martha gave Matt a warm bath, thinking about how she would discuss McCann and Devlin with her husband. She hadn't seen any papers and didn't know what the articles had said. Maybe this was the reason he seemed so distant.

After Matt was in bed and asleep, Martha fixed tea and brought it to the front porch. Jacobson was pointing to a hardwood rocking chair.

"This is yours, Martha. I bought it especially for you."

Martha sat down. "It's wonderful, Blaine. I guess you haven't forgotten how well I like rockers."

"No, I haven't. I just hope you can spend a lot of leisurely time there."

"What do you mean, Blaine?"

"It's this matter concerning the jailbreak in Cimarron. I'm not worried about you being indicted for a crime. We'll say that you were kidnapped by those two men. That was the case, wasn't it?"

"Actually, I broke them from jail," Martha admitted. "But I'll certainly say that I was kidnapped. There's only one man alive who can say that I did it voluntarily. He's a killer who works for Marvin Hurlan."

"Are you certain of that?"

"I couldn't be more certain, Blaine. His name is Carlton. He and a number of others would have killed me had they gotten the chance."

"Hurlan is well thought of in these parts," Jacobson said. "It would be hard to make people believe something like that."

"You believe me, though, don't you, Blaine?"

Jacobson sipped his tea and looked out over the city. "Yes, Martha, I believe you."

"I hope you aren't actually considering working for someone like Hurlan."

"I intend to look into it."

"Blaine, you can't be serious. Didn't you hear what I just told you? That man is vicious!"

"Have you met him?"

"No, but I have perfectly good word on it."

"Perfectly good word? From two outlaws?"

"They aren't outlaws, Blaine. They're very decent men."

"Then how did they end up in jail?"

Martha stood up and walked over to her husband. "You know how that happens, Blaine. You, better than anybody, should know that there are a lot of innocent people behind bars."

"Martha, can you really vouch for their innocence? It surprises, indeed shocks, me to know that you risked your own life, not to mention our future, breaking two strangers out of jail."

"They weren't exactly strangers."

"I'm sorry! I don't understand."

Martha described how McCann had had a letter from her father. She told further how McCann had been searching for his wife and son and that she couldn't leave him and his friend behind bars when she knew they hadn't done anything wrong.

"It just wasn't right to leave Cimarron and know that Trent and Ruz were going to kill them. I just couldn't do it."

"I know you have a noble heart, my dear," Jacobson said, "and that's an honorable trait. But it can get you into serious trouble at times. In this case, very serious."

"I thought you said it would be easy to say I was kidnapped."

"Oh, that won't be difficult. It's just that the whole process will be sticky. That's all. It will be sticky for you and, let's say, a good advertisement for me."

"Good advertisement?"

"Yes. Don't you see, when word gets out how good I am in court, I'll have more clients than I'll know what to do with. I won't even have to go to the gold fields to strike it rich. I'll just bill those who've already gained their wealth."

Martha sat back down in the rocker, fighting tears. "I was afraid of this, Blaine. You've come up here and the smell of big money has clouded your thinking. Do you know now why I wasn't excited about you coming here? We were perfectly content down there. If you hadn't left, none of this would have happened."

"Oh, now you're blaming me for your escapade with the outlaws."

"I told you, Blaine, they aren't outlaws!"

Matt appeared in the doorway. "I heard you talking. You're loud."

Martha rose. "Don't worry, Matt. Everything is fine."

"Why were you yelling?"

"Mother is very tired. You know that. It's been a very hard trip. Maybe I should take a nap with you."

Matt cheered up. "You can sleep good. I sure did until you woke me up."

"You run along back to bed," Martha told him. "I'll be right in."

When Matt had left, Martha turned to her husband. "I don't know if I can be happy here, Blaine. Certainly not if you go to work for Marvin Hurlan. I can't imagine that."

Jacobson was standing at the edge of the porch, watching travelers on a distant road. "You'll be happy here, Martha. You just have to give it time. And you have to change your thinking a bit."

"That's just it, Blaine. I can't change my thinking. I don't want to."

"Why don't you go and see to Matt? Rest for a while. You're right, you're very tired. Maybe rest will help."

"Are you still going to meet with Marvin Hurlan?"

"I told him I would. I can't very well go back on my word."

"Blaine, I wish you wouldn't."

Jacobson turned and placed a hand on her shoulder. "Martha, I think you're overreacting a bit."

Martha glared. "You refuse to listen. I don't think you even believe me."

"There's a man coming very soon to escort me up. I'll be gone for one night. I'll be back by early afternoon tomorrow."

Martha turned away.

"You know, Martha, you're going to have to get used to this," Jacobson said. "Important clients demand attention."

"I thought the clients were supposed to come to you."

"They will, in time. But I need to hook a few big fish first. Then the rest will follow."

"Have it your way, Blaine." She left the porch for Matt's bedroom.

Matt had already gone back to sleep. Martha lay down and pulled him close, feeling the hot tears on her cheeks. She felt like a stranger in someone else's house. She certainly didn't feel like Blaine Jacobson's wife.

She had known things would change the day he had first talked about going to the gold fields. He had insisted. When he had left, she had known that nothing would ever be the same. Now it was happening, only it was going to be worse than she had thought.

Twenty-Three

McCann sat in Devlin's cabin in Central City, reading newspaper accounts of the incident in the Molly Jordan. He and Devlin had taken a couple of days to discuss strategies against Hurlan while the Cornishmen cleaned the loose rock out of the tunnel.

Hurlan had told the press that it had been an accident, that miners in the Molly Jordan who had been setting off a blasting charge had somehow misjudged the fuse length.

Penrose and the other Cornishmen were harboring a lot of anger. They had gone down into the deep shaft and had retrieved the remains of their friend. One of the miners injured in the blast had died, and the other was near death.

Penrose and the others had decided not to dispute Hurlan's story. Instead, they had decided to go to work as if it had been an accident. They had their own ways of getting even.

"I'll bet Penrose talks every one of Hurlan's men into quitting him," Devlin predicted. "Hurlan's got a bad reputation as it is. Soon they will see the error of their ways and sign on with us. Don't you think, lad?"

"It appears as if he's got a good start already," McCann remarked. "Penrose was saying just this morning that he's got a lot of Hurlan's men talking about quitting."

"I didn't hear that, lad. When did he say it? In fact, I didn't even know he was here."

"Oh, he was here, with about ten other miners."

"No."

"Yes, he was." McCann laughed. "You were sleeping, Corky. You ought to get to bed sooner at night."

"You mean you had a meeting this morning without me?"

"No, you were here, Corky. But you were too busy snoring to take part."

Devlin threw a wad of dirty socks at McCann, who ducked them and turned to the second page of the paper. He frowned deeply. "Look at this," he told Devlin.

The paper contained an article about a Denver lawyer who had been killed in a fall from his horse while on his way to Central City. The accident had happened two days previously. The lawyer had come to Denver from Cimarron, New Mexico, and had been a promising legal counsel for the prominent men of the area.

"That's Martha's husband!" Devlin said. "Lord God in heaven!"

The article described how Blaine Jacobson had died after being thrown from his horse, falling over the edge onto the rocks below the Smith Hill Road. According to an eyewitness, a man named Jensen who had been traveling with him, Jacobson's horse had shied at a snake and he had died at the scene.

"A man named Jensen was with him," McCann said. "I wonder what Hurlan's trying to do."

"He's aiming to get rid of the lot of us, one by one," Devlin said. "He's hiring killers, I'd say."

McCann read further, learning that interment was to take place the next morning in a Denver cemetery.

"I wonder if Martha's gotten to Denver yet," Devlin said.

"I should think so," McCann said. "She's had a lot of time to get here. Maybe we should head to the cemetery."

"I've seen too many burials lately, lad," Devlin said. "It makes my heart sick to think about the boy, Matt. He's bound to be taking it hard."

McCann thought about the other boy back along the trail, the son of the redheaded woman. He still hadn't gotten over that.

"I'll agree with you," McCann said as he strapped on his Colt, "there's been too much dying. And it's all because of one man. I think it's time we put an end to it."

There was a small crowd at the cemetery, for few people had gotten to know Blaine Jacobson that well. Martha was off by herself, with Matt by her side, watching a priest pray over the coffin.

McCann and Devlin waited until the prayers were finished. The priest said a few words to Martha and left her staring into the grave as workers lowered her husband.

McCann and Devlin approached. "I'm sorry, Martha," McCann said. "I read about it this morning."

"Thank you for coming," Martha said. "I wondered if you had learned of Blaine's death, or if you had even made it into this area. I wish now that I hadn't."

Matt looked up. "I'm glad to see you, too. I wish none of us had ever gone from home down in Cimarron." He bit his lip.

Devlin squatted down and began talking to Matt. "It's all right to feel bad, you know. You don't have to hold it."

Matt was staring. "I don't think this would have happened if Mother and Father hadn't been yelling."

"Oh, you can't say that, lad. You can't blame anybody. I know you don't understand. But nobody does. It's the Lord's will."

"Sometimes I get mad at the Lord," Matt said. He began crying and fell into Devlin's arms.

McCann walked with Martha toward another tombstone. It bore the name of a man who had died the year before in a similar accident on Smith Hill.

"A woman was out here at this grave earlier," Martha said. "She came over and told me that her husband had been a lawyer, too, and had learned something about Marvin Hurlan. "Why can't somebody stop this man?"

"He's about finished," McCann said. "Who was the man with your husband on Smith Hill?"

"I didn't get to see him. I was in the bedroom with Matt. I know I should have gotten up, but I was angry. I asked Blaine not to go, but he wouldn't listen."

"Are you saying Hurlan had invited him up to Central City?"

"Blaine was going to work for Hurlan. That's what he told me. But that was a setup. Now Blaine's dead and I'll likely go to jail for breaking you and Corky free."

"I wouldn't worry about it," McCann said. "There would have to be witnesses that actually saw you break us out. There are none besides Carlton, and he's not credible. A decent lawyer could twist him in knots. Besides, all you have to do is say that we kidnapped you."

"That's what Blaine told me," Martha said. "He was a good lawyer, but he wanted too much too quick. Hurlan played him like a fiddle."

"What are your plans now?" McCann asked.

"I haven't thought about that yet. I don't know if I want to stay here. But I can't go back to Cimarron. I just don't know."

"If you stay here, you're going to have to be careful, you know," McCann said. "Hurlan might be after you, also."

"Why would he be after me?"

"Because you're the only one left who can testify in our behalf. There's a federal marshal after me, and if he catches me, I'm going to bring Hurlan into the mess. You're the only one left who knows what's happened."

"What do you suggest I do?" Martha asked.

"We met some Cornishmen along the way with ties here in Denver and Central City," McCann said. "We'll have them watch your house and keep an eye out generally."

"That would make me feel much better," Martha said. "Did you ever catch up with your wife?"

"It wasn't my wife." McCann told her about finding the man digging the grave for his murdered wife, and how she had so closely resembled Minnie. "I'm still shaken by it. There's no way to know where Minnie is now, or if she and my son are doing well or not."

"There's so much trouble for small children," Martha said. "It's too bad there isn't some place they can go for help when they lose their parents."

Matt came back over to his mother. He was wearing Devlin's red derby.

"Mr. Devlin says I'm a strapping young lad. He says I'll do fine. What are we going to do now that Father's dead?"

"We'll make it, Matt," Martha assured him. "I know you're confused and worried, but things will work out for us."

"Mr. Devlin said he would show me his mine one of these days," Matt said. "He said he might even give me some gold."

"Mr. Devlin is a nice man and he'll do things with you, if you want him to," Martha said.

"He wants me to call him Uncle Corky. Is that all right?"

"Certainly," Martha said, "if you'd like to."

Matt thought a moment. "He doesn't really look like an uncle. But maybe he is."

Devlin leaned over. "And just what does an uncle look like, lad?"

"I never saw an uncle with a red hat before," Matt said.

"Well, I'll bet you can get used to the hat if you wear it enough," Devlin said.

Matt studied the hat. "Maybe. When are you going to take me to your big gold mine?"

"I'll give you a couple of days with your mother," Devlin said. "Then I'll take you up there and we'll have the time of our lives. You can even stay the night at the cabin if you'd like."

Matt turned to his mother. "Could I?"

"I don't see why not," Martha said. "It would be good for you, I think."

Matt suddenly stopped and stared. At the edge of the cemetery, a carriage came to a stop. A large man got out, and another man dismounted from a palomino horse.

"The big one is Marvin Hurlan," Martha said. "I've seen pictures of him."

"The one with the palomino must be Jensen," McCann said, "the man who was with your husband."

"Of all the nerve!" Martha said. "What are they doing here?"

Hurlan walked over, flanked by the rider, who was also dressed in a business suit. McCann studied them both, not liking what he saw.

As Hurlan approached, he removed his hat. "I'm sorry, ma'am. You have my deepest sympathy."

Martha looked the other way.

"Your husband was to have dinner with me," Hurlan continued. "He was a fine lawyer. It would have been good to have him work for me."

"What is it that you want, Mr. Hurlan?" Martha asked. "I find it hard to believe that you're offering me your sympathies."

"Well, ma'am, that is why I came."

McCann noticed Hurlan's partner eyeing him. Though dressed neatly, the man had a very hard edge to him. McCann could tell that he'd spent more time outdoors than in. His hands and face had seen a lot of weather and his fingers twitched, especially near the butt end of his Colt.

Hurlan leaned over and patted Matt on the head. "He's a fine boy. He needs a place where he can grow up safely."

Devlin took Matt by the hand. "Let's go pet the horses, lad. There's an odor here that's hard on me nostrils."

When Devlin and Matt were gone, Martha said, "I'll ask you once more, Mr. Hurlan. Why are you here?"

"Actually, Mrs. Jacobson," Hurlan continued, "I would like to inquire into your home. I don't know what your future plans are, but if you've been thinking about selling . . ."

"No, Mr. Hurlan," Martha said. "I don't think so."

"I could give you a more than fair price."

"You must be hard of hearing," McCann told Hurlan. "The lady said she wasn't interested in selling to you."

"I beg your pardon?" Hurlan said.

"If she wants to sell," McCann said, "she'll get in touch with you. How's that?"

"You must be Mr. McCann," Hurlan said. He made it clear that he had no intention of shaking hands. "I've heard a great deal about you. You might have made your way up here in good stead, but you're in unfamiliar territory now."

"You're forgetting, Mr. Hurlan," McCann said, "I worked this area before the war. Mr. Devlin and I have a very good claim, right next to yours. I'm sure you're aware of that."

"Yes, of course," Hurlan said with a twisted grin. "Then perhaps you and I should be talking business. Do you suppose?"

"What business did you have in mind?"

"Perhaps you and Mr. Devlin would consider selling the Molly Jordan."

"No, I don't think we would," McCann said. "I know I'm safely speaking for Mr. Devlin as well."

"I would reconsider if I were you," Hurlan said. "I would give you a more than fair price."

"Not interested."

"Then you'll have to settle for nothing. Perhaps you've heard of the apex law of common lode mining."

"We've heard of it," McCann said. "And we've discovered that a vein that starts on our claim goes down underground into your claim. So, under the apex law, I guess we'll be crossing over into your property and legally taking over your claim. Thanks for opening the tunnel for us."

Hurlan turned red. He glared at McCann and replaced his hat. "I can prove otherwise, Mr. McCann. I know a number of prominent geologists and metallurgists. You would be very foolish to try and beat me in court."

"Our lode is a rich one," McCann said. "We can keep up with you financially. We'll be in court for however long it takes to beat you. Just try us."

"You had better take my offer, Mr. McCann," Hurlan said. "Otherwise, you and Mr. Devlin may not be mining for much longer."

McCann watched him leave, his hired gunfighter trailing close behind.

"That man will stop at nothing, will he?" Martha observed. "I'd say he would have had his gunman try and kill you right here if he'd thought he could get away with it."

"Hurlan would do anything if he thought he could get away with it," McCann said. "Right now he's getting desperate. A lot of his miners are quitting him to go to work for us. He won't be getting away with anything from now on. His time has about run out."

Twenty-Four

Carlton stood just inside the entrance to the Molly Jordan, waiting for Devlin and Matt to arrive. The midafternoon sun was shining warm, but the hillside was quiet.

All of Hurlan's miners had left and were organizing with Penrose and the Cornishmen. Carlton had taken time to organize himself, to set things up the way he wanted to. He had made some decisions, and it was time to follow through on them.

Now things were happening fast. Carlton knew he had to work quickly and smoothly to get everything accomplished. He had figured it all out, and the thought of getting McCann was foremost in his mind.

Getting McCann was all he could think about. Carlton was certain that Hurlan intended to have Jensen go after McCann by himself. Carlton couldn't let that happen.

As far as Carlton was concerned, Jensen didn't have the right to go after McCann, whether or not Hurlan had hired him. It wouldn't be right or proper. Len had been *his* brother, not Jensen's. If Hurlan had just allowed them to work as equals, as he had promised, things might have been different.

And now time was running out. He had to get McCann before the following morning, when the Cornishmen were set to begin work. If he didn't have McCann by then, it would be too late.

With his spyglass, Carlton had been watching Devlin ride up the hill, holding Matt in front of him. Carlton began to smile. Devlin's afternoon with the boy was not going to be what he had expected.

As Devlin neared the mine, Carlton ducked back inside. He could hear Devlin joking with the boy, telling him how they would mine some big nuggets and take them back down to his mother.

Carlton waited until Devlin and Matt had gotten well inside the tunnel. Then he grabbed Matt and clamped his hand over the boy's mouth.

"For the love of God!" Devlin said, raising his hands. "Do what you want to me, but leave the boy be."

Devlin cocked his pistol and placed it against the side of Matt's head.

"You'll do just what I ask, won't you, Mr. Devlin?"

"What is it you want?" Devlin asked. "McCann's not with us."

"I know that. But I'm going to make things so that he comes up here to visit."

"Just let the boy go," Devlin said.

"Not just yet," Carlton said. "I'm going to tie you both up and leave you here for a while. I want you both to sit quiet until I get back. If something happens that you're not here when I get back, I'll find the boy and dump him down the long shaft. Is that understood?"

"We'll be here," Devlin said.

Carlton tied a gag around Matt's mouth. The boy stood still, trying not to cry. Carlton then gagged Devlin and tied them to a mine timber.

"You rest comfortable now," Carlton said. He grabbed Devlin's red derby. "I'll take this with me. It'll come in handy."

It was late evening, just past twilight. Carlton had ridden down from the mine and was eager to meet with Hurlan.

Carlton parked the wagon in back of Hurlan's mansion, where he always did, and walked around to the front. He entered by the front door and was taken to Hurlan's office by the butler.

Carlton stepped into the room. Hurlan and Jensen were talking by the light of a lantern on Hurlan's desk.

Hurlan turned and glared at Carlton. "You're late."

"My horse threw a shoe."

"You've always got some excuse, Carlton. Did you bring the wagon for the girls?"

"It's in the back."

Hurlan seemed satisfied. "Sit down. We've got some plans to discuss."

Carlton seated himself. Hurlan ignored him while he talked to Jensen about McCann.

"I want you to be extra careful," Hurlan was saying. "The man is way better than most. Do it right."

Carlton felt the anger well up within. Jensen had

no right to go after McCann. Hurlan had no right to order him.

"Mr. Hurlan," Carlton broke in, "I don't believe I've had the pleasure of meeting this man. I mean, we've talked a number of times, but I've never officially met him."

"Oh, is that so," Hurlan said. "Is it that important to you?"

"Yes, if I'm going to be working with him."

Hurlan removed his cigar and said, "I want you to stop this insisting, Carlton. I'll tell you what you're going to be doing and when."

"Could I just meet him anyway?" Carlton squeezed his hat and stepped toward Jensen.

Hurlan stared at Carlton. "Why is it so important?"

Carlton felt his heart pounding. He hoped no one could hear it but him. Jensen was smirking.

Carlton came within five feet of Jensen and stopped. He took his right hand from his hat and pulled the Colt from his belt, cocked it, and fired. The surprised Jensen took the blast full in the chest, falling sideways off the chair.

Carlton cocked the pistol and turned it on Hurlan, who sat numbed in his chair. He had just started to rise, putting his hand in front of him, when Carlton fired.

The bullet blew the cigar to shreds, clipping off Hurlan's forefinger and part of his thumb. Carlton's second shot took Hurlan high in the chest, shattering his collarbone.

Hurlan gasped and slumped back down in his chair. Carlton stepped over and put another bullet into Hurlan's forehead.

Jensen was lying faceup on the floor, his eyes

Colorado Gold

half-open. He seemed to be breathing, so Carlton shot him in the head.

Carlton wanted to rejoice, to stay and drink Hurlan's liquor and yell that he was no longer a coward. He had done it! He had fired straight on!

But Carlton had no time to waste. He dropped the pistol and hurried to the third floor. He fumbled with the keys and finally unlocked the door that held the chained women.

They were both semiconscious. One of them stared at him blankly. He lifted her and threw her over his shoulder, hurrying down to the first floor.

In Hurlan's office, he propped her up against the front of Hurlan's desk, next to Jensen's dead body. He got the pistol and fitted it to her hand, while she continued to stare blankly.

"That's good," he said to the woman. "There's one shot left. Aren't you sorry you did all this?"

Carlton raised the pistol to her temple and cocked the hammer back. Her eyes suddenly changed, widening, but Carlton ignored it.

He pulled the trigger, using the woman's own finger. Her head slammed back against the desk and she slumped sideways to the floor, letting her hand fall, the pistol still in her grip.

On his way out, Carlton took the lantern from Hurlan's desk and threw it against the wall. Flames and liquid rolled down and across the floor, filling the room with smoke.

Carlton left by the servants' entrance and jumped into the wagon. He was out into the street and two blocks down when he heard the shouting. He looked back and saw a lot of people running toward the big mansion, now alive with fire.

Twenty-Five

The night was calm, with a nearly full moon rising. Martha stared at the sky for a while, then came in from the porch. With Matt spending the night in Central City, it was a good time for thinking about the future.

She slipped out of her dress and settled into a steaming tub of bathwater. It should have relaxed her more than it did, but so much had happened in so short a time.

She had finally begun to think about what to do with her life. Blaine's death was still very fresh in her mind, but she had to start making some decisions. He had accumulated a good deal of money since coming to Denver, which would now go to her, but that wouldn't last forever.

And she didn't want to sell the mansion. It was a beautiful home with a lot of space. It could certainly be used to house mothers and their children who needed a temporary residence.

Martha had come to the conclusion that she wanted to be a social worker. She wanted to help women who had lost their husbands in the mines, or by any other means, until they got their lives back in order. She knew that in many cases, she would be caring for homeless children. She believed that with so much wealth in the area, she should be able to get some contributions toward her cause.

As she wondered how she would start her endeavor, she thought about Matt. He would surely be having a good time with Devlin up at Central City. Looking forward to seeing the mine had been a good diversion for him. It was nice to have someone like Corky Devlin who would spend time with him.

Martha washed her arms, remembering how it had felt to be without Matt during the time she had ridden from Cimarron with McCann and Devlin. It made her feel a little lonely. Matt was now all she had in life.

And McCann, having had to go through what he did in finding the murdered woman. If he weren't so determined to find his wife, just maybe . . .

Martha stopped washing. She thought she had heard a creaking board just outside the bathroom. It gave her a strange feeling.

She thought about Hurlan and Carlton, and the advice McCann had given her to be careful.

She heard the creaking board again and held her breath, staring at the doorway.

Carlton eased into the bathroom, his pistol drawn, his other hand behind his back.

"My, but ain't you pretty."

Martha grabbed her towel from a chair beside the tub. "What are you doing here?"

"I've come to take you for a ride."

"I'm not going anywhere with you."

"Yes you are. That is, if you want to see your little boy alive."

Martha's stomach tightened. "What are you talking about?"

"Your little boy. He's up at the mine," Carlton said. "He misses you. He wants to see you."

"You're lying. You don't have my son."

Carlton took his other hand from behind his back and threw Devlin's red derby on the floor near the tub.

"Now, are you still going to call me a liar?"

Martha gasped. "What have you done with him?"

"He's fine. But like I said, he won't be if you don't follow my orders."

"What do you want?"

"I told you, we're going for a little ride, you and me."

Martha's thoughts were racing. She had no way to be sure he hadn't harmed Matt already. It was likely he had injured or even killed Devlin to get the boy. Devlin wouldn't let Matt go without a fight.

"How do I know that my son hasn't been harmed?"

Carlton smiled. "You don't. But you're coming with me anyway, aren't you? You don't have a choice."

"Where do you want me to go?" Martha asked.

"You don't need to worry about that."

"I have to see my son. I have to know that he's all right."

Carlton stepped forward and yelled, "You don't *have* to know anything until I say so! Do you understand?"

"Yes, I understand. Just give me a minute to get dressed."

"How about if I watch."

"I'd rather you didn't, if you don't mind."

"I think I will anyway." He smiled crookedly.

With no choice, Martha stepped from the tub, the towel wrapped around her. She held the towel in place with her chin and pulled the dress down over her head.

"Hurry up!" Carlton hissed. "I haven't got all night."

"I need to find something for my feet."

"No you don't." He shoved her out of the bathroom and toward the door.

Beside the door was a bottle. Martha assumed it was one Carlton had been drinking from. He popped the cork and handed it to her.

"Take a long swig."

"I don't care to, thank you."

"I didn't ask you if you cared to. I said do it." He glared at her. "Remember your little boy?"

Martha took the bottle and tipped it. It didn't taste like whiskey. It tasted more like a red wine, heavily sweetened. She handed the bottle back to Carlton.

Carlton insisted she keep it. "More. I want you to drink it to here." He put his finger a third of the way down the bottle."

Martha drank two long swallows and handed the bottle back to Carlton. She almost gagged.

"You'd better keep it down," Carlton said. "You'll just have to drink more. Here, another drink."

Martha didn't argue. She gulped another mouthful.

"See, that wasn't so bad." Carlton was smiling. "Now, just sit down in this chair."

Martha felt her legs growing weak. She hadn't even gotten into the chair when she was aware that Carlton had thrown her over his shoulder and was carrying her out the door. Her eyes wouldn't stay open. He was laying her in the back of a wagon, covering her with a tarp. It was black underneath. All black.

Devlin sat in the mine with Matt. His hands ached where the ropes were tied, but he had long since stopped struggling against them.

He had also stopped trying to talk to Matt. The gag in his mouth was too tight for him to make words. He could only hope that the boy was all right.

It seemed like an eternity since Carlton had jumped them and had left them bound. Devlin knew it had to be late at night by now.

He wondered why McCann didn't think something was wrong and come up to check things out. He had told McCann that he and Matt would be back in time to cook a deer steak for supper. It was way past suppertime now.

Maybe something else had happened. Maybe McCann had come up to check on them and Carlton had bushwhacked him. There was no way to know anything. He would have to sit with Matt in the darkness and wait.

Matt moved a little, struggling again to get himself free. Devlin had heard him crying earlier. Then he had been silent.

Devlin felt helpless, unable to do anything, even to help Matt in some way. Someone should be coming soon.

He was thinking again about McCann when he heard footsteps in the tunnel. It was Carlton, and he had Martha with him.

Carlton held the lantern in Devlin's face. "Did you think I'd forgotten you?" He laughed. "I'm going to untie you and I want you to be polite."

Carlton removed the gag from Devlin's mouth. "What in the name of God are you up to?" Devlin asked. "How could you leave a little boy tied up like this?"

"You just sit and listen," Carlton said.

Martha was on her knees, bound and gagged, her head bent over. She appeared sleepy and incoherent. Matt had come alive at seeing her, struggling at his bonds, but Carlton left him tied.

"What about the boy?" Devlin asked.

"He can stay right where he's at. You, on the other hand, are going to find McCann."

"How would I know where he's at?"

"I'm just saying that you'd better find him," Carlton said. "You had better look hard. And when you find him, you'd better make him understand that I want him to come up here." He pointed to Martha and Matt. "Tell him to hurry or these two will take a bad fall down a very deep mine shaft."

"McCann could be anywhere," Devlin said. "It could take a day to find him, especially if he's gone down to Denver."

"It had better not take a day to find him," Carlton warned. "It had better take just a few hours. You'd better hope he didn't go to Denver."

"I can't know that," Devlin said.

"I want him here before first light," Carlton said. "I don't want any miners coming in here before he gets here. If it gets light and a lot of workers show up, they'll never see these two. They'll be a long ways down below. Tell McCann that. Hurry, Devlin. Hurry and tell that to McCann."

Twenty-Six

A nearly full moon had climbed high into the night sky. McCann was riding up the trail toward the Molly Jordan. The cover of darkness made him feel somewhat better, but not much.

McCann had gone to Denver to check on some gold samples he had left at the assay office, but he had stopped short in the doorway. Inside was a federal marshal, talking to the employees, holding up a wanted poster with his name and face on it.

McCann had hurried away, then had followed the marshal at a distance. The marshal had begun tacking the posters up everywhere.

The picture of McCann on the poster had been taken at the end of the war, when he had posed in uniform with some other soldiers. It wasn't a good likeness, with the heavy beard. That was the only thing McCann had going for him.

McCann had then left for Central City, only to learn when he had gotten there that the marshal had arrived shortly after him. Penrose and a few of the Cornishmen had come to the cabin to warn him. They had stayed at the cabin to try and put the marshal on a wrong trail.

Meanwhile, McCann had had to leave the cabin and occupy himself in some way until the marshal left town. The marshal hadn't left, but had spent the afternoon drinking in the saloons, talking to people, and riding back and forth to the cabin.

McCann had wanted to leave for the Molly Jordan earlier, but had decided against it. Devlin had taken Matt up for a good time. McCann knew that had he ridden up there, and had the marshal suddenly arrived, it could have been a bad situation.

Then, just after sundown, McCann had gotten his chance to come out of hiding. Marvin Hurlan's mansion on Eureka Street had gone up in flames. Everyone in town had gathered, including the federal marshal.

McCann had been curious about Hurlan's misfortune, but couldn't stop to find out what had happened. He had wanted to tell Devlin that he would soon be leaving the area.

McCann had found no one at Devlin's cabin. Devlin and Matt were supposed to have been back in time for supper. McCann had wondered if something had happened to them at the mine.

It was then that McCann had made a decision. He had written his thoughts on two different pieces of paper and had then sealed them in separate letters.

One he had slipped under his mattress, the other he had put in his pocket.

McCann had headed toward the mine, wishing he had ridden up sooner. Now he was thinking, as the moon rose higher, that a lot of things could have happened to Devlin and Matt. His mind was churning through them all.

His biggest concern was that they had somehow fallen down the long shaft, or that some large rocks from the earlier blast had come loose from the ceiling and had injured or killed them.

McCann could only wait until he got there. Even then he wasn't sure what he could do if they were badly injured. But by morning Penrose and his Cornishmen would be up to begin work and they could help. Just so the marshal didn't arrive.

As late as it was, McCann had passed no one on his way up. It surprised him when he saw a rider hurrying down the trail toward him.

McCann eased his horse over a ways and lowered his head. The rider passed him at a trot, then turned his horse back. McCann drew his Colt.

"McCann? Is that you, lad?" Devlin called. "Thank the good Lord I found you."

"Where's your derby?" McCann asked. "Where's Matt?"

Devlin told how Carlton had jumped them early in the afternoon, and had left them tied the rest of the day and half the night.

"Carlton showed up again just a little while back," Devlin said. "He had Martha with him. I don't know how he got her, but she's tied up and he's threatening to throw her and the boy down the long shaft if you don't get up there."

"There's another problem, besides," McCann said. "A federal marshal has showed up and he's tacking wanted posters with my picture on it all over the gulch."

"Oh, God in heaven!" Devlin said. "There'll be men a-sprouting from the hills looking to gun you down."

"For some reason, they aren't after you," McCann said.

"I can't figure it either," Devlin said. "God above knows I'm not always an angel. But what are you going to do, lad?"

"I'll have to leave," McCann said. He pulled an envelope from his pocket. "I've decided to sign my half of the mine over to you."

"You can't do that, lad."

"It's for the best," McCann said. "I can't stay around here. You do what you think is right with the money that would have been mine."

"Are you thinking about Martha and Matt?"

"I wasn't sure if you were alive or dead when I wrote up the paper," McCann said. "Since you're alive, you'll get the mine in full. You can make your own decisions."

"You can be sure I'll help Martha," Devlin said. "Matt says that she's talked about keeping women and children on who've lost their fathers in the mines."

"That would be a good cause," McCann said. "There should be plenty for that. No more time for talk."

"I'm going back and help you with Carlton," Devlin said.

"He would expect that," McCann said. "We can't take the chance."

"Then maybe I can stall this marshal that's looking for you," Devlin suggested.

"That would help me the most," McCann said. "I'll go on up to the mine and hope that I can sneak up on Carlton."

"However you do it," Devlin said, "you'd best be careful. If anything happened to either Martha or Matt, I just couldn't take it."

Martha felt more helpless than at any other time in her life. The mine was hot and damp, the floor rough and uneven. She had mostly recovered from the drug that Carlton had put in the wine, but she was groggy and her feet hurt. She worried about twisting an ankle or knee in the loose rock of the mine floor.

Carlton held a lantern in front of him. He herded her along, impatient, yelling at her when she stumbled.

"Take the blindfold off then," she insisted.

"It's not time yet," Carlton told her. "You just keep up if you don't want me to whip you with this rope."

Carlton was carrying extra lengths of rope over his shoulder. She could only think that he intended to tie her up somewhere.

Carlton continued to push her, telling her how he was going to make Joel McCann sorry that he was ever born. "He shouldn't have killed Len," he repeated over and over. "He shouldn't have killed my brother."

Martha kept quiet, working to keep her balance. It seemed as if he was taking her to the middle of the earth, as if they had been descending forever.

Finally Carlton stopped. He jerked her forward and she went to her knees.

"We're here," he said. "Too bad you can't see."

"Take the blindfold off. Please."

"Maybe, if you talk nice and promise to do anything I ask you to do."

"What do you mean?"

Carlton laughed. "We don't have to be bored while we're waiting, now do we?"

Martha could feel him sitting down beside her. He removed the blindfold.

"Say thank you, now."

Martha tried to focus her eyes. "Are you going to untie me?"

"Not yet."

Martha saw his crazy smile, his face coming closer. Suddenly his lips were crushing hers. She tried to turn away, but his hands held both sides of her head.

"Ah, that's nice," Carlton said. "Let's do it some more."

From the distance came the sound of Matt yelling. Carlton tensed, then broke into a broad smile. That's why he had left Matt tied up alone in the darkness. He had known that Matt would start yelling when he heard someone coming.

Martha rubbed her bruised lips with the back of her hand, tasting blood.

"You hear that yelling?" Carlton said. "Your little boy has just told me that McCann's on his way."

Martha remained silent.

Carlton shook her. "I know you heard the yelling.

Mr. McCann's on his way back. Soon to be dead Mr. McCann."

"How do you know it's him?" Martha asked.

"It's him. Who else would it be?"

"It could be anyone."

"No, it's McCann. You and I both know it's McCann. Devlin found him right away, just like I knew he would."

Martha sat quietly, listening, hoping it was McCann and that he would hurry and take her away from this madman. She had felt good at hearing Matt's voice, knowing he was all right, but she wanted to be free of Carlton in the worst way.

Carlton settled next to her and blew out the lantern. He peered back down the tunnel, whispering, "Come to me, McCann. Come to me."

Carlton drew his Colt. There was no sound, none at all. Carlton grew impatient. He yelled into the darkness, "McCann, I know you're there! Come here and let's finish this."

No answer. No sound.

Carlton leaned over and whispered into Martha's ear. "I want you to scream. Loud."

"No."

"I said scream!" Carlton hissed, jamming his pistol into her ribs.

"You scream," Martha said.

"So you don't want to scream," Carlton said. He tied a length of rope around her middle and secured it to a timber. He forced her to sit on the edge of the shaft.

"Do you feel like screaming now?"

Martha sat still and tense, her legs dangling over the edge. She couldn't move or she would fall into the shaft. She knocked a rock loose which tumbled downward, bouncing off the walls, until it splashed into water far below.

"Why don't you just push me and get it over with?" Martha asked.

"Oh, no. That wouldn't be any fun," Carlton said. "We've got to get McCann down here, too. He's going over the edge with you. Now, I want you to scream, so he knows you're here."

"I'm not screaming," Martha said.

Carlton gave her a shove. Martha dug her fingers into the sides, trying to keep herself from falling. Carlton pushed her again and she slid off the edge.

The rope caught her fall. She dangled, helplessly, swinging back and forth in the tunnel.

Carlton was above her, yelling, "Now do you feel like screaming? I want to hear you. Do it! Do it or I'll cut the rope!"

Martha could hear Carlton's yelling echoing in the shaft around her, his voice falling past her, bouncing off the walls. She could feel the rope moving above her and she was certain he was cutting it, like he had promised.

With all her might she opened her mouth and screamed.

"That's better," Carlton said. "That's much better."

Twenty-Seven

McCann had been cautious upon entering the mine. He hadn't known where Carlton had taken Martha or what to expect. He had lit a match only occasionally, for a quick moment, to see where he was. Otherwise, he had crept forward in darkness.

Near the entrance to the side tunnel, he had heard Matt crying and yelling, "Who is it? Who's there?"

McCann had untied him and had held him close. "Everything's going to be fine, Matt."

"No, it's not," Matt had sobbed. "He's got my mother. He took her back there, to the big hole in the ground."

"I'm going back there and get her," McCann had said. "I want you to stay here and be extra quiet. Do you understand?"

"I'm tired of being alone."

Colorado Gold

"I know. But it will only be for a short time more. Can you handle it?"

Matt had nodded. "Where's Uncle Corky?"

"He went down into town. He'll be back before long. Maybe you could wait at the entrance for him."

Matt had agreed and McCann had helped him back to the entrance. Moonlight had been showing down and Matt had said, "I wish Mother was with us."

"She will be soon," McCann had promised. "You stay right here and wait. It won't be long."

McCann had made his way back cautiously, knowing that Carlton had taken Martha to the deep shaft. As he had started into the side tunnel, he had been able to hear Carlton talking to her.

McCann had made his way forward by groping at the timbered walls. Straining his patience, he had crept to within fifteen feet of Carlton and Martha. He had wanted to fire at the sound of Carlton's voice, but didn't dare. Martha was right next to him, defying his every move.

Now Carlton had pushed her over the edge, and he was yelling into the shaft at her. He had gone nearly berserk with rage.

McCann lit a match, blew it out, and rolled to the other side of the tunnel. Carlton opened fire, streaks of flame bursting from his pistol, illuminating himself.

McCann opened fire on Carlton. Carlton yelled and dropped his pistol into the open shaft, then slid over the edge.

McCann scrambled forward, hitting his knee against the lantern. He lit it quickly and peered down into the shaft.

Martha was ten to twelve feet down, groaning. Like a crazed monkey, Carlton was hanging on to her for dear life.

Martha had heard the gunshots, deafeningly loud in the closed space of the mine. She had felt Carlton's pistol bounce off her shoulder and had heard it clatter down into the darkness. Then Carlton had come over the edge, yelling, cursing, reaching for anything he could grab on to.

He had taken hold of her rope, sliding, clutching her by the head and shoulders, his breath ragged. Now his weight against her was nearly suffocating.

She screamed, "Let go!" but he clung all the harder, cursing McCann, his breath rasping in her face. He struggled against her, trying to climb out.

Above, the timber that held the rope began creaking. A light shone down into the shaft. McCann was there just as the timber began to pull free. He grabbed the rope, holding with all his might.

The weight of Carlton on top of Martha was nearly too much for her. She couldn't breathe. Carlton was clutching the rope ever harder, strangling her.

Martha tried with all her might to push him off. She pushed on him and pulled on his clothing. She kicked off the side of the shaft, slamming him into the opposite side. But he was holding with his last dying strength, his blood soaking her dress.

McCann held fast, the rope burning his hands. He braced himself against the opposite side of the shaft, pushing back with his legs. The timber creaked louder. When it finally gave, he would go down with Martha and Carlton.

Colorado Gold 215

Lanterns and the sounds of men's voices gave him added strength. If he could just hold on until they reached him.

Martha again kicked off the side of the tunnel, once more slamming Carlton into a timber. Carlton groaned. His head began to sway from side to side. He slipped down, his bloody chest smearing her forehead. His eyes, huge, met hers.

"I'm gone," he choked. "Gone."

His fingers loosened their grip and he fell downward into the darkness without a sound, his body bouncing off the walls, finally hitting the water far below.

Martha gasped for breath. She felt herself being pulled upward and over the top. She lay in the rocks with McCann leaning over her.

"Can you hear me?" he asked. "How are you hurt?"

"No," Martha said, breathing heavily. "It's not my blood. Carlton's. Where's Matt?"

Devlin had just arrived with Matt. He jumped toward her. Martha took him into her arms, tears streaming down her face.

"Thank God you're safe," she said. "Thank God."

"You're all bloody," Matt said.

"It's not my blood," Martha said. "You don't have to worry about anything anymore."

Penrose and the other miners arrived and crowded close. Penrose stood over McCann and laughed. "You don't need the likes of us fer nothing. I wish you would stick with us and not be leaving. You could do all the bleddy mining yourself."

"I'd like to stay," McCann said. "But that's not possible."

"What?" Martha said. She sat up. "Where are you going?"

"There's a federal marshal in the area," McCann explained. "He's likely on his way up here right now."

"More to the point, 'ee's on 'is way into the mine," Penrose said. "The boys are a-trying to keep 'im back, but 'ee will be 'ere any bleddy minute."

"That he will, lad," Devlin said. "I'll be taking you out another tunnel, where Mr. Penrose showed me."

McCann followed Devlin, with Martha and Matt close behind. Devlin led them through an adjoining tunnel that connected to Marvin Hurlan's property.

"This will soon be part of the Molly Jordan," Devlin said, as they neared the entrance. "A nod of thanks to the common law of apex mining." He laughed.

Outside, the morning sunshine shone brightly over the mountains. Some of the Cornishmen were waiting with McCann's horse.

Devlin told McCann and Martha the story involving Hurlan's mansion fire.

"There's going to be some cover-up, there will," Devlin said, "but I figure there was a shootout of some kind. The fire burned them all to ashes, though. No one will ever really know the truth."

"I want the truth about Trent and Ruz to come out," Martha said. "And their connection to Hurlan." She was speaking directly to McCann. "It's not fair that you have to leave."

"I don't want to have to shoot another federal

marshal," McCann said. "Anyone with a badge is considered in the right."

"You wire me once in a while," Devlin said. "I'll let you know when it's clear."

Martha stood a way back, Matt at her side. She was fighting tears.

"I wish you didn't have to go," Matt said.

"Can't be helped," McCann said. He wanted to step over and take Martha in his arms. He held back.

"We're going to miss you a lot," Martha said. "You've done a great deal for us."

"Corky will fill you in on the mining profits," McCann said. "Maybe you can start on your plans sooner than you had hoped."

"Will you ever be back to share in them?" Martha asked.

McCann mounted his horse. "I can't say. I hope so."

"You listen to me, lad," Devlin said. "You let us know where you are and what you're doing. You hear?"

"I promise," McCann said. "Take care of yourselves."

McCann rode up a back trail that would take him over the mountain. Devlin stood below with Martha and Matt, waving. They got smaller and smaller in the distance.

At the top of the divide, McCann stopped and looked back down over the gulch. He didn't know where he would go or what he would do, but he would find his way back, someday. Meanwhile, he would dodge the law and go where the mountain winds took him.

WESTERN ADVENTURE FROM TOR

☐	58459-7	THE BAREFOOT BRIGADE *Douglas Jones*	$4.95 Canada $5.95
☐	52303-2	THE GOLDEN SPURS *Western Writers of America*	$4.99 Canada $5.99
☐	51315-0	HELL AND HOT LEAD/GUN RIDER *Norman A. Fox*	$3.50 Canada $4.50
☐	51169-7	HORNE'S LAW *Jory Sherman*	$3.50 Canada $4.50
☐	58875-4	THE MEDICINE HORN *Jory Sherman*	$3.99 Canada $4.99
☐	58329-9	NEW FRONTIERS I *Martin H. Greenberg & Bill Pronzini*	$4.50 Canada $5.50
☐	58331-0	NEW FRONTIERS II *Martin H. Greenberg & Bill Pronzini*	$4.50 Canada $5.50
☐	52461-6	THE SNOWBLIND MOON *John Byrne Cooke*	$5.99 Canada $6.99
☐	58184-9	WHAT LAW THERE WAS *Al Dempsey*	$3.99 Canada $4.99

Buy them at your local bookstore or use this handy coupon:
Clip and mail this page with your order.

Publishers Book and Audio Mailing Service
P.O. Box 120159, Staten Island, NY 10312-0004

Please send me the book(s) I have checked above. I am enclosing $ _____
(Please add $1.25 for the first book, and $.25 for each additional book to cover postage and handling.
Send check or money order only—no CODs.)

Name _____
Address _____
City _____ State/Zip _____
Please allow six weeks for delivery. Prices subject to change without notice.